SABELA

"*J*'m going to miss you."

Davin took my hand and held it gently. There was a sadness in his slate-grey eyes. "I'm going to miss you too."

He wasn't making this any easier.

"Are you sure this is what you want?" he asked, swinging his flight-bag over his

shoulder.

"It's not what I want. It's what we *both* want. We both knew you'd be going off to

university, six months after moving in together. We've known for months that we'd be going our separate ways eventually."

Davin glanced up at the monitor displaying the flight schedules in the terminal at San Diego Airport, where we stood. His legs were crossed at the ankles, like they always were when he stood for long periods of time. I had to admit, he looked sharp in his beige pants, matching short-sleeve cotton shirt, and loafers. His short, dusty-colored hair, neatly combed back. There was no doubt I was going to miss him, but I had prepared myself for this moment, when he would leave Southern California to study at Rice University in Texas to become a doctor.

I'd spent most of my twenty-four years here in the San Diego area, where I worked as a dental assistant.

My mom, who was now alone after Dad died last year from an unexpected heart attack, was only an hour away.

Yeah, it's going to be tough to come up with the entire rent for our one-bedroom duplex close to the beach, but I'd manage. I'd get a second job if I needed to. I wasn't about to pack it all in to follow him to Texas. We'd only been dating for a few weeks before we decided to move in together, and it was more of a convenience to help each other out before he was to move away in August. Call it a "friendship with benefits."

W e met through his younger sister, Claire, who also worked at the dental office, as an x-ray technician. When Davin came in as a patient one day, we hit it off. That evening, after my shift, we met for coffee and things developed from there.

"Flight number 287 is now boarding at Gate twelve," echoed through the terminal from the loudspeakers above us.

He uncrossed his legs and stood straight. "That's my flight. I gotta go," Davin said, while searching my eyes for any second thoughts. He wrapped his arm around my waist and gave me a tender squeeze. "You can still go with me. It's not too late, you know."

I unwrapped myself from his hold. "No, I can't, Davin. My life is here, and yours will now be in Texas. You take care of yourself, okay? Keep in touch."

He gripped my waist again and pulled me in. "One last kiss?"

I laughed and rolled my eyes. "Sure."

He moved his hand to the crook of my neck and curled his palm over my shoulder, then kissed me one final time. It was a warm, tender kiss that lingered longer than usual. But it wasn't enough to make me surrender and follow him like a lost puppy. I was okay with us parting. Another chapter was about to close in my life and it was time to begin a new one.

Our lips parted and Davin let me go. "Bye, Sabela. It's going to be hard to give you up. I've grown quite fond of you."

I blushed at his confession but thought nothing of it. "By the time you land in Texas, I'll be a distant memory." I ushered him with my hands. "Now, go on, before you miss your flight."

I watched with mixed emotions as he walked toward the gate. Doubts began to enter my mind. *Am I doing the right thing? Should I run after him?* Shaking my head, I quickly pushed away the conflicting thoughts and allowed Davin to walk out of my life. Before disappearing into the crowd of other passengers, he stopped, turned to face me, and waved. I reached my hand high above the crowds of people and waved back, not allowing my misty eyes to turn into full-blown tears

The drive back to the duplex wasn't easy. Returning to an empty home was even harder. As I walked through the now silent living room, all of Davin's things gone, I wished we had bought that puppy we talked about so many times before. I needed to be greeted by a wagging tail and slobbery kisses to ease the sadness I was feeling.

I slumped my body onto the beige couch and stared up at the ceiling, allowing the circular motion of the fan to hold my attention. I embraced the moment of silence to gather my thoughts and accept the fact Davin and I were no longer a couple, and it was for the best. I've never believed in long-distance relationships, and I was certain, in no time at all, he'd meet some cute, young student and forget all about me. I didn't need that possibility held over my head. I was still young—I had my whole life ahead of me and Davin's life was not for me. Especially in Texas.

After mulling on the couch for what was probably close to an hour, I changed into my favorite cut-off frayed denim shorts and a white t-shirt. Wearing my white bikini underneath, I decided to pull myself together and head for the beach. I needed some sunshine right now and the beach always lifted my spirits. It was only two blocks away, and a place Davin and I had visited often.

Being a weekday and early afternoon, the beach was relatively quiet. The sun was already high in the sky, welcoming me with beaming rays of heat. Just a few surfers lingered in the water, sitting on their boards, waiting for that perfect wave. I noticed a few couples and groups had found their spots on the sand and set up camp for the day.

I didn't feel like being around people, so I found a secluded spot at the edge of the beach, where the sand met the rocks. I claimed my space and laid out my towel.

I gave the beach one more scan before removing my shirt. I stopped and did a double-take. To my left, about fifty feet away, sat a gorgeous looking guy. With his wetsuit peeled down to his waist, his bronzed muscular chest and well-defined abs were exposed for me to appreciate in all their glory.

"Where did he come from?" I mumbled to myself. Not wanting to be caught staring, I reached into my purse, grabbed my large-framed sunglasses, and put them on. Now shielded behind my shades, I took another look, trying to play it off like I was simply enjoying the view.

Which I most certainly was.

"Is he watching me?" It felt like he was looking right at me as he faced my direction, a surfboard lying next to him. He must have just gotten out of the water because his thick head of dark wavy hair was dripping with beads of ocean water. I took a deep breath —this guy had my attention, and the fact that he was watching me too, stirred something inside.

CHAPTER 2

SLATER

*S*he knew I was looking at her. Hell, every guy on the beach probably was. How could anyone not? My eyes zoned in on her the minute I left the water. That body was perfectly toned in all the right places. Those thigh muscles, clearly defined as she walked across the sand. Her long, straight, black hair, swayed gently in the breeze as it cascaded down her back. I stopped at the edge of the water and enjoyed the view.

My eyes followed her as she had made her way toward the edge of the beach. I'm sure I was drooling. I watched as she bent down to spread her towel across the sand, admiring her cute little butt in those tight denim shorts that accentuated every little curve. It took every bit of willpower I had not to march right on over there and pinch it.

"Damn, she's hot," I whispered under my breath, while enjoying the rise between my legs. I needed to make sure my eyes weren't playing tricks on me. After unzipping my wetsuit and freeing my arms, I picked up my surfboard and found a spot closer to her. Oh, she was gorgeous all right. She reminded me of some Brazilian goddess with her natural olive skin. I couldn't tear myself away, I was so captivated by her beauty.

I caught her glancing my way and had to chuckle when she put on her shades. I knew she was using them to sneak a second look at me. *Does she like what she sees? I wonder if she's single?*

I quickly scanned the beach for any male walking her way and was pleased when I saw no one. But that didn't mean anything—she may have a man at home.

Fantasies of our bodies entangled together began to enter my mind. I could feel my manhood begin to stir, which could be somewhat embarrassing while wearing a wetsuit. I tried discreetly to calm it with my hand but it continued to fight back. I eventually gave in and casually laid my hand in my lap to hide the now noticeable bulge.

This was my first time on this beach and if that gorgeous woman is a regular here, then I can guarantee, it won't be my last.

It was the first thing my surfboard and I did when I moved to a new town—checked out the local beaches. Working in construction, I followed the jobs. When the crash of the stock market, and then the fall of the real estate business happened a few years ago, finding work had been a struggle at times. So, when this job came up, I jumped on it and rented a room in the area last week. I didn't mind moving from place to place. It's how my life has been ever since Eve left me, almost three years ago. In a matter of ten hours, my world had been crushed and turned upside down.

We'd been together since high school. I was sixteen when I met her at the school dance. I noticed her right away from across the large hall. She was standing with a group of girls, giggling and talking. Their squeals could be heard across the room – which is what got my attention. She was the tallest and was wearing a red satin dress that hugged her slender body. Her thick, long blonde hair glistened under the lights. She saw me and smiled, our eyes locked, and that was it. The rest is history.

I fell hard for Eve. She was my everything and there was

nothing I wouldn't do for her. I gave her my all, working ten to twelve hours a day so she could stay home and concentrate on starting up an online business. I lived, loved, and breathed Eve. When we were nineteen, we rented a house and moved in together. Even though Eve's mother, Patricia – who was widowed the year before when Eve's Dad died from lung cancer – objected profusely. I was never good enough for Eve, according to her mother. Eve and I talked of marriage, buying our own home, and starting a family. My life was on track with plans and goals to achieve and I couldn't wait to see what the future held for the two of us.

Five years later, when I was twenty-four, she left me. I came home one day after work and she was gone. She had taken all her belongings. Only my clothes hung in the closet and only my things remained on the bathroom counter. I found a handwritten note on the kitchen counter, telling me how sorry she was and that she had met someone else.

After running through the house, checking every room in disbelief, in the hopes of finding her, my heart felt like it had been shredded into a million tiny pieces. For hours, I sat in the corner of what was once our bedroom, shocked and numb to the core. It was the only time I had ever cried and I didn't even have a photo of her to hold while my tears shed – she had taken them all. Which I found odd.

After my heart, could ache no more, anger began to replace the hurt. Questions began to enter my mind. Who was the guy? Where did she meet him—my guess was online while she was supposed to be conducting yet another business. Ever since I'd known Eve, she had this dream of becoming a successful internet entrepreneur. I lost count of how many start-ups she'd had. Every one failed miserably and cost me a bunch of money, but I kept supporting her to keep her happy.

I soon realized, she must have been planning this great move of hers for months, and the worst part was, I never saw it coming. I was so busy being in love with her and believed she felt the same way, I was oblivious to any signs she was having an affair and falling in love with another man.

In my fury, I had torn up the note and thrown it on the floor. I didn't want to be in that house anymore, grabbed what stuff I had, and left, promising myself my lips would never say her name again. Eve had ripped out my heat and taken it with her. I'd been on the road ever since and never saw her again. I never spoke of her and to me she was now a distant memory.

Since being dumped by Eve, I'd stayed clear of dating anyone seriously. I wasn't ashamed to admit it—I was afraid of having my heart broken again. I had the occasional one-night stand, which was all I needed right now to satisfy the urge to feel a woman in my arms, even if it's only meaningless sex. Yeah, I wasn't gonna lie, it would be nice to meet someone special again, settle down, and have a woman to share my life with, but it was hard to meet someone when you traveled from town to town like I did. And here I was again, in a new town, where I reckoned I'd only be for about six to eight months, depending how long the job lasted.

It's a big housing track job and should provide me with an income for a while. I've got an orientation in about an hour, and the job starts tomorrow, bright and early, at seven in the morning. I guess I'd be getting my surfing time in on weekends after today.

I glanced down the beach again. Damn, I didn't want to go to any meeting today. No woman had ever captivated me like the beauty I was looking at right now, not since Eve destroyed my world. How was I ever going to pull myself away?

Oh, there she goes. She's reaching for the sky with the bottom of her tank top in hand. I held my breath in anticipation of seeing more of her smooth, delicate skin. I stared intently, refusing to blink. I was already hard and could feel myself about to explode. I gave my now prominent erection another discreet massage to calm it down. In one swift movement, she pulled her shirt over her head and flung it to the ground, followed by a sexy shake of her hair. I swore she was looking straight at me and smiling as she tossed her hair to one side. But it was hard to tell with those damn shades on.

Man, she's gorgeous. That tiny white bikini top she was wearing didn't leave much to the imagination. My eyes zoned in on her perfectly full, round breasts, barely hidden by the light delicate material that accentuated her natural dark skin.

I continued to watch intensely, not taking my eyes off her. I didn't care if she knew. It looked like she was enjoying the attention anyway. I swore she was teasing me. Why did I think that? Because she wasn't removing her shorts right away. Every move she was making was slow and provocative, directed solely at me. I sat with my mouth gaped open, while she adjusted her little top over her breasts. I held my breath as she reached inside the thin material and cupped each boob in her hand, positioning them just right inside her bikini. Oh, how I wish I were that hand. I'd be giving each nipple a tender squeeze right about now.

With a full-blown hard-on, I had to continue to calm it with the palm of my hand, and I practically drooled with lust while watching her pull her hand out of her top and push both breasts together in a flirtatious manner, followed by what I believed to be a subtle seductive smile. I glanced quickly at her full, voluptuous lips. Thoughts of kissing them entered my mind, escalating my heart into full-on racing mode.

My gaze traveled down her stomach, stopping at her belly button. She was fit, her abs clearly defined through her skin. I imagined it was smooth to the touch and pictured my hands invading her body, caressing every inch with deep rubs, while tasting her salty skin with my tongue. Itching to touch her, my palms and fingertips began to tingle. I clenched my fists tight and buried them in the sand to fight the urge.

After what seemed like a lifetime, she eventually moved her hands toward the button of her shorts. I held my breath again with anticipation. "Oh yeah. Come on, baby," I whispered to myself.

Before popping the button, she raised her head and glanced my way. Yeah, she definitely knew I was watching. I was sure of it. Again, my manhood began to throb. I squeezed it while enjoying the view. After undoing the button to her shorts, she slowly slid the zipper down, revealing the sexiest V to the treasure between her legs I had ever seen. I could taste it now. With my eyes about ready to pop, I watched as she grasped the top of her shorts and with slow, sensual moves, wiggled her perfect little body out of them. My eyes followed as she pulled them down over her thighs, past her knees, and over her calves. Curling her toes, she gracefully stepped out of her shorts and let them fall onto the sand.

"Wow!" I said, a little louder than I intended to. I wonder if she heard me? If she did, she didn't seem to mind. She had taken my breath away. Her long, toned legs glistened in the sun. Oh, how I would love to spread them and bury my face between her thighs. I bet she would be the sweetest thing I'd ever tasted.

I knew I should be getting some more surf time in right about now. It was getting late in the day and the waves would be laying down soon, but I was glued to my spot. I couldn't peel my eyes away from the magnificent sight before me.

Then, when I thought it couldn't get any better, she bent over purposely in my direction, giving me a full view of her perfectly round backside, and pulled out a bottle of suntan oil from her purse. I even caught her sneaking a peek at me between the space of her arm and body. She probably wanted to make sure I was still watching.

I grinned at what lay ahead. "Oh, this should be good."

CHAPTER 3

SABELA

I couldn't believe I was doing this and actually enjoying it. Never in my wildest dreams had I ever thought I'd enjoy being watched by a stranger. What a rush this was. Every nerve in my body was on fire and I didn't want this new sensation I was experiencing to end. I'd never done this before and never thought what such a turn-on it could be. Then again, I'd always come here with Davin and never paid much attention to anyone around us. We never flaunted our affection in public either—that was always kept to the privacy of our bedroom.

Suddenly, my mind flashed back to Davin. I left him at the airport less than two hours ago and now here I was, flirting with another guy. A guy I didn't even know. But Davin had always been so conservative. I never realized it until now. Sex had always been the same boring missionary style, with no passion and no words exchanged. Most of the time, after he had come, we were done. There were no fireworks, no affection, or cuddles afterward. It was flat and we did it because we felt we should. Well, looking back, that's how I perceive it now, I just never realized it at the time.

I always believed I was somewhat shy and reserved when it came to sex. But then, I'd never had the opportunity to express myself and explore my wild side. Hell, I never knew I *had* a wild side. But something inside of me had been unleashed and it felt friggin' awesome. What I was doing felt pretty wild and I suddenly felt liberated.

Knowing I was this guy's object of desire was such a boost to the ego, I just went with it. I blocked everyone else out, imagining it was only me and him at the beach. I wanted this guy to want me and it seemed like my flirtatious moves were working. He hadn't taken his eyes off me the whole time. Thank god I put my shades on; I didn't want him to see I was looking back. But man, he was gorgeous. I couldn't help noticing the bulge in his wetsuit either and had to chuckle when he tried to hide it with his hand. Seeing that was truly gratifying. I knew he liked what he saw. I wanted to tease him some more—the fire within me had been ignited and I wasn't ready to put it out just yet. I was having way too much fun. It was at that moment I decided to reach for my suntan oil.

After giving him a full view of my behind—which I knew he would appreciate—I took a seat on my towel and prepared myself to coat my now tingling body with the warmed coconut oil. I was loving the power I held over this guy. Knowing he was anticipating my every move was so uplifting.

Peeking from behind my shades, I studied him as I slowly removed the cap from the bottle. His body shifted as he placed his hand again over his noticeable erection. I smirked with satisfaction, then shook my head to toss my hair to one side and applied a generous amount of oil to my legs. I watched as it trickled over my skin and down my calves. Seducing me with its warmth, I slowly began to massage the oil into my legs with the palms of my hands. Using long strokes from my toes to my thighs, I rubbed my skin deeply, coating every inch, making sure to brush across my crotch with my fingertips. The subtle touch with my fingers made my hungry core ache for attention.

Before moving up to my stomach, I took another glance at my audience. He was still with me, both hands clenched between his legs. I poured another generous amount of oil over my protruding breasts and middle. I released a small gasp as I felt the liquid my body. I watched as it trickled down, soaking the inside of my top and over my nipples. With my nipples now hard, I closed my eyes and began to rub the oil tenderly over my front.

Visions of the stranger's hands stroking my skin entered my head as I caressed my breasts and gave my nipples a slight pinch. I parted my legs slightly. The cool breeze that swept up between them was a welcomed sensation, cooling me down a notch. I swear, if I wasn't on a public beach, I could bring myself over the edge with no problem. But I resisted by giving the space between my legs the occasional brush with my hand as I continued to knead the oil into my skin, admiring how it glistened in the sun.

My body itched to be touched by the man sitting down the beach from me. Thoughts of him tracing my curves with his lips and tongue caused me to lie back and arch my spine just a touch. I was feeling liberated and wild, like I had just released the animal from the cage. I could never remember a time when I had felt so turned on and I was loving it.

With my back slightly arched, I opened my legs a little wider and reached inside the front of my bikini bottom. The material surrounding my core was soaking wet. I was yearning to be filled. I caved in and gave myself a quick poke with two fingers, to satisfy its needs. I gasped yet again before removing my hand.

I imagined the stranger approaching me and satisfying me completely, with no words spoken. I didn't want this moment to end but the sound of my phone ringing from inside my purse crushed that idea. Frustrated, I yelled, "Damn it!" *Who the hell was calling me? Should I answer it?*

In a split second, I went from total ecstasy, floating in the clouds with the discovery of a new sexual empowerment that touched the core of my body, in a way I had never experienced before, to being what I could only describe as flatlined. In a snap, I was instantly brought back down to earth. The mood had been broken with no hope of it returning. Reluctantly, with a harsh jerk of my arm, I sat up and reached for my purse.

Whoever was calling had such bad timing and better have a damn good reason. After a few seconds of digging through my purse and following the sound of the pestering ring, I located my phone and yanked it out. Davin's picture was flashing on the screen. "Davin? What the hell does he want? We've already said our goodbyes," I whispered under my breath. Unable to hide the anger I was feeling, I answered with a sharp, "Hello."

"Sabela! I couldn't wait for the plane to land, so I could call you."

"What? You're still on the plane. What's up? Why are you calling?"

"Yes, we just landed and I realized, while in the air, what a huge mistake we are making. I miss you and we should be together."

The tone of his voice was creeping me out. I pivoted onto my rear end so

my back was facing my recent desire, and curled my body over the phone. I spoke with a harsh whisper. "What are you talking about? We already said goodbye. There's no way we can be together. We talked about this, Davin."

"Oh, but we can, sweetheart. Just pack up your things and come to Texas."

Sweetheart? He's never called me that. "No, Davin! I'm not moving to Texas. My life is here and you know that. Why are you doing this?"

"You don't mean that. It's only been a few hours, but soon, you'll miss me as much as I miss you. I'm not going to let you go, Sabela. You're mine, and always will be."

Chills rushed through my body, causing the tiny hairs on the back of my neck to rise.

"Davin, you're freaking me out. I'm not yours. I never was. You don't own me. You're—"

"Oh, but you *are* mine, Sabela," Davin cut me off. His voice had a sudden threatening tone. "Trust me. You will come to Texas and I'm not giving up until you do. I'll be in touch."

The phone went silent. I was left looking at the now-blank screen with a feeling of uncertainty. What the hell just happened? Tons of questions raced through my mind. What's gotten into him? He can't be serious? Puzzled, I shook my head and tried to blow it off as Davin just going through some emotional breakup crap.

Suddenly, I remembered the cute guy and turned in his direction. My heart sank, he had left. I scanned the beach but he was nowhere in sight. "Well, thank you, Davin," I mumbled under my breath as I reached for my shorts, deciding to call it a day and head home.

CHAPTER 4

SLATER

*W*ell, dammit! As soon as it started getting good, she gets an effin' phone call. I waited for a few minutes with an aching hard-on, hoping it would be a quick call and we could resume where we had left off. I sat patiently, but as soon as she turned her back, I knew the incredible experience had ended.

Disappointed and still with a raging hard-on, I pulled my wetsuit over my arms and zipped it up. I grabbed my surfboard and decided to take one last dip in the ocean before heading to my scheduled meeting.

When I got home, I had less than an hour to take a shower and change. The shower took longer than expected. Reflecting back to what had happened at the beach, I had to relieve myself and boy, was it good. I hadn't come that good in a long time. But after the affair with myself, I realized what an idiot I had been. Why didn't I stick around and approach her? Or get her number, at least. God, I hoped I'd see her at the beach again. What were the chances, I wondered? The image of her was permanently imprinted in my brain. If I was lucky enough to see her again, I wasn't going to let her get away next time, that's for sure.

After an intense shower, my body felt drained and I felt somewhat lightheaded. I forced myself to get dressed and head over to the job site, which, thank god, was only ten minutes away.

It was the usual boring meeting giving the crew the rundown of the job at hand. One hundred fifty units were to be built within the year. I was the slate tile guy—hence the nickname, Slater. I was one of the best in the business and had earned quite a reputation. Sure, I'd be doing other tasks on the job—framing, drywall, et cetera—but when it came time to lay the tile, I was the guy.

Drew, the man in charge, was also someone I considered to be a good friend. We'd worked on many jobs together and he tended to keep me in the loop when something new came up. He kept me busy when Eve left me and listened like any good friend would do, when I had no one to talk to and needed to empty my heart. Drew had his life in order and lived the life I hoped to someday—a wife, a couple of kids, and a nice home. I'd always thought about taking my career to the next level and taking on my own jobs. I had my contractor's license but I wasn't ready to take on the responsibility of being in charge.

I tried to stay focused at the meeting, but it was hard. I didn't know how I was going to get through the week, or weeks, for that matter, without seeing that girl. I decided I'd keep going to the beach until she showed up. Something told me she lived around here. When she left, she didn't head toward the parking lot; instead, she kept walking down the beach. That told me she lived within walking distance of where I saw her. Man, I was stupid to leave. I kept wondering who called her on the phone. Whoever it was, she didn't look too happy to hear from them. I saw the frustration and anger written all over her face when she answered the call. What if she *did* have a boyfriend? But then again, she was clearly flirting with me. She knew damn well I was watching her and I knew she was loving every minute of it.

CHAPTER 5

SABELA

I was feeling pretty creeped out after talking to Davin. His voice sounded different, almost threatening, but he just didn't seem the type. I'd spent almost six months with him, and not once did he ever raise his voice at me. He always seemed like the shy, quiet type. The Davin I had just spoken to on the phone wasn't the Davin I knew. What had gotten into him? *I was his. I will move to Texas.* Who the hell does he think he is? I couldn't help wondering though, if I had a reason to worry? I instantly shook my head, erasing such silly thoughts, and laughed at myself. *Nah. He's all the way in Texas. What could he possibly do?*

Back at my duplex, my body felt tense, thanks to anger directed at Davin. I tried to brush it off by taking a warm bath. As I submerged my body into the welcoming water, the stresses I was feeling began to disappear. "Ahh," I said out loud as I laid back and closed my eyes. I reverted my thoughts back to the beach, and the images made me smile.

I still couldn't believe what I had done. In some way, I felt like a naughty, dirty girl—but in a good way. I giggled at my confession. My friends would be shocked if they knew what I had been up to.

Shit, I couldn't tell anyone. If word got back to Davin's sister, Claire, she'd for sure tell Davin. No, this was going to be my little secret.

Damn! I wished he hadn't left. Friggin' Davin had to ruin everything. I had just discovered the joys of being watched and now it was being overshadowed by Davin's weird call. God knows what would have happened if he hadn't called. I wonder if the guy would have approached me? And would we have made out? I had a distinct feeling we would have.

Fantasizing about what may have happened was sending electrifying sensations through my entire body. Reminiscing the scene at the beach, I reached into the warm water, spread my legs a little, and began caressing myself. I melted from my touch, and buried two of my fingers deep inside of me. I gasped at the sudden gratifying sensation as I began to feed its need of being filled. Picking up speed with my legs spread wider, I moved my fingers in and out of my throbbing core while caressing my breasts tenderly with my other hand. An orgasm was within reach.

Suddenly, I heard the ringing of my phone come from the other room. I tried to ignore it and continued with my quest, attempting to shut out the annoying ring tone. It stopped and I let out a sigh of relief. I was almost there. *Come on. Think back to the guy at the beach.* I switched back to my erotic thoughts, only to be interrupted by my phone again.

"Damn it!" I yelled, frustrated as hell. "Not again!"

With the mood now broken once more, I slapped the surface of the water with both hands, pulled myself out of the tub, and wrapped myself in a towel.

Still dripping with water, I hurried into the living room and located my phone, only to be greeted by Davin's picture on the screen. "Seriously!" I yelled, before answering. I was unable to hide my annoyance in my voice. "What now, Davin?"

"Are you packed yet?"

I shook my head in disbelief. "Packed? No, I'm not packed. I already told you, I'm not coming to Texas."

"And I already told you that you are. This is no joke, Sabela. I always get what I want."

I could tell by the tone of his voice he wasn't joking.

With uncertainty in my voice, I spoke in a calmer tone, "What's gotten into you, Davin? You're acting crazy. I can't come to Texas. My life is here. Now, can we stop this nonsense?"

He snarled at me through the phone, "No, you listen to me, Sabela. I'm not playing games with you. Do you understand? You're going to pack your things and get your fucking ass on a plane to Texas, or you suffer the consequences. Do I make myself clear?"

Then the line went dead.

"Davin?" I looked at the blank screen, speechless. *Consequences?* Fear swept over me. This wasn't the Davin I knew. Still wrapped in my towel, I moped around the apartment, unsure what to do. *What consequences is he talking about?* I tried to brush it off, but his threat haunted me for the rest of the night. Feeling uneasy, I turned off my phone, dressed myself in my favorite *Hello Kitty* pajamas, then curled up on the couch with a blanket and pigged out on popcorn and soda while watching old black-and-white movies for the rest of the night.

CHAPTER 6

SABELA

*T*he next morning, I woke with a splitting headache, worried about Davin and what he may be capable of. I thought I knew him, but last night, he showed a side of himself that was freaking me out. I decided, from now on, I wasn't going to answer any more of his calls, and if he continued to press me about moving, I would change my number. But for now, I had to hustle and get ready for work.

With a new attitude toward Davin, I drank two cups of coffee, along with downing a couple of Tylenol to ease the throbbing in my head, and quickly got dressed in my dental assistant scrubs, grabbed my purse, and headed out the door to what was now my car.

Davin might be acting weird, but as I fired up his old Toyota Camry, I had to be thankful he gave it to me before he left. My old Volkswagen bug was on its last leg and was making all kinds of strange banging and clanging noises. I'd made plans for Pick-A-Part to pick it up at the end of the week because I didn't have any extra money to fix it. Davin surprised me a few days before his departure by handing me the keys to his black Toyota and telling me it was mine. It was no skin off his nose—his parents paid for everything, including his apartment in Texas, which they wanted him to have so he wouldn't have to sleep in a dorm inside the university, and he would be getting a new car.

When I arrived at work, I thought about talking to Davin's sister about his unusual phone calls, she never spoke to me much and I think it's because she didn't like me dating her older brother. She'd probably side with him and think I was crazy. So, I decided against it and kept my fears to myself.

Much to my relief, the rest of the week zipped by without another phone call from Davin. It seemed life was back to normal and I was worrying about nothing. He's probably settled in by now and I hoped as I cross my fingers, he had met someone else and forgotten all about me. God, I hoped that was the case.

A day hadn't gone by this week without thoughts of the guy from the beach continuing to invade my head. Good thoughts that made me smile. I couldn't get him out of my mind. I planned on going back to the beach this weekend, in the hopes of seeing him again. If I do, then what? Should I approach him? Shit! I didn't know. I didn't want to come across as too forward. But damn it! I also didn't want to let him go a second time.

The weekend couldn't come fast enough. As soon as Saturday rolled around, I packed my things for the beach, with enough supplies to last the whole day, if necessary. I plan on hanging out, in the hopes the mysterious stranger would eventually show up.

I arrived early, around nine and took the same secluded spot as last time, hoping he would show up, looking for me. I laid out my towel and began undressing down to my bikini—which, by the way, wasn't as hot as last week when I was being watched by the cute guy. As I peeled off my clothes, I found myself scanning the beach, with the hope I would spot him watching me. But I came up disappointed. *God, I hope he shows up.* I so wanted to see him again.

Before making myself comfortable on the towel, I checked the beach one more time, to no avail. I did notice a couple of single guys looking my way, but they didn't interest me. Only one guy would get my attention and sadly, he wasn't here.

The sands were quiet. Just a few people were soaking up the rays of the sun and about a dozen surfers were sitting on their boards in the ocean. I squinted my eyes to see if one of the surfers was the stranger but they were all just a blur. *It's still early,* I convinced myself. *I'm going to wait here all day if I must.*

CHAPTER 7

SLATER

"Oh fuck, there she is!" I almost fell off my surfboard the minute I saw her. Even from out here, sitting on my board waiting for the next wave, I couldn't miss her. My heart instantly began pounding like a hammer. She was just as beautiful as I remembered. I spotted her as soon as she stepped on the sand and gracefully walked over to the familiar spot. *What do I do? I don't want to scare her off. Come on, Slater. Think!*

I sat on my board for quite a while, missing some good waves, contemplating what to do next. The minute she started to undress, my cock began to stir. Even from this distance, she turned me on. I didn't want to mess this up. I'd been thinking about seeing her again all week, but I hadn't thought about what I was going to do if I actually did. I couldn't remember a time I'd been so hung up on a woman, not since Eve. This girl had me by the reins and was pulling me in from every direction.

Was it just my imagination or wishful thinking? It sure looked like she was looking for someone before she made herself comfortable on the towel. If she was, I hope it was me.

I couldn't think straight anymore. My mind was all twisted

with sexual fantasies and at the same time, I was asking myself, what do I do now? It was a jumbled mess. I needed to think. The next big wave was going to have to crash against the shore without me. I had to go for it. I wasn't going to let her slip away this time

Like a hunter going in for the kill, I paddled back to shore on my board and headed her direction, not taking my eyes off her. When I got within twenty feet of where she was, I stopped to catch my breath. The weight of my board was taking its toll on me. I tried to calm my breathing—the combination of fatigue from walking across the sand and the excitement from being so close to her had me gasping for air.

"Man, she's beautiful," I mumbled to myself as I admired her lean body stretched out on the beach, soaking up the sun that was beating down on her immaculate body. She was lying on her back, wearing the white bikini I remember so well. Her arms were straight, with her palms face down on the towel. My gaze wandered down to her legs, which were perfect and slightly apart. I zoned in on the sensual space between her thighs. Heated from the sun, I yearned to bury my face between them and taste her warm juices.

My sinful thoughts were causing my breathing to escalate even more. I needed to calm myself. "Settle down, Slater. Just get your ass over there and take it from there." I took a deep breath and headed for my target. She didn't move. She had no idea I was approaching her. I continued to mumble, "What do I say to her? Fuck! What if I've been wrong this whole time, and she thinks I'm some sort of pervert and didn't enjoy me watching her?"

I shook my head. *Nah. I saw her looking my way. She was enjoying it as much as I was.*

Convinced, I took the final steps toward her towel and stood in silence, admiring all her beauty. She was just inches from my touch and my cock knew it. I calmed it again with my palm and waited for her to stir.

CHAPTER 8

SABELA

I didn't know where he came from, he just suddenly appeared. I felt my cheeks flush as I raised my hands to block the sun and I saw it was the guy from last week. There he was, standing before me in all his glory. His handsome face was smiling at me, peaking my nerves. He must have just come from the water. He was dripping wet, wearing a wetsuit—this time, zipped up—and carrying his surfboard under his arm. His thick dark hair, coated in beads of water, was a tangled mess, but it just added to his sexiness. Strands of it glistened in the sun, catching my wandering eye. I found myself tongue-tied, hearing only the erratic pounding of my heart beneath my chest. For the past week, I had hoped for nothing more than to see him again, and now here he was.

There was an unnoticeable silence between us. Unsure of what to say, I waited for him to speak first.

After what seemed like an eternity, he finally did. "Hi. I hope I'm not bothering you. I saw you here last week, and thought I'd come over and say hello."

A brush of embarrassment flooded through me when he mentioned our first encounter, and the thoughts and fantasies I had of him back then began to resurface. My skin tingled from the rush of heat surging through my body. Every nerve was on fire, yearning to be touched by this man. "Hi," I said nervously. "Yeah, I remember." I said, trying to sound as casual as possible.

He chuckled at my confession while thoughts were rambling off in my head: *Of course I remember you. How could I not? I've only been thinking about you all week.* He leaned forward and extended his hand. "I'm Slater, and you are?"

No longer partly shadowed by the sun, his handsome face came into full view and I was mesmerized. My heart skipped a beat as I was drawn into his dreamy ocean-blue eyes that were locked with mine. His face, with its prominent square chin, with a sexy five o'clock shadow, and his defined cheekbones, was the color of bronze, tanned by the hours he probably spent surfing. His voice couldn't be any more masculine. It was deep and had a rough edge that made my toes curl. I couldn't help myself and threw him a flirtatious smile as I took his wet hand into mine. He had a strong grip—his skin rough. His touch shot a whirlwind of sparks through me. I spoke as calmly as I could, considering the circumstances. "Hi, I'm Sabela."

He smiled back. "Hmm, Sabela. What a beautiful name. I love how it rolls off my tongue."

I laughed. "It's Portuguese."

"Well, Sabela, would you mind if I became the envy of all the other guys on this beach and joined you." He paused and smiled again. "You do know that every guy around here is watching you? Can't say I blame them. You're absolutely stunning."

I quickly scanned the beach and took notice. He was right, several curious sets of eyes belonging to a cast of single men were staring our way.

The realization stirred something inside of me, bringing me

back to when I was being watched by Slater last week. It was the same kind of foreign excitement which ignited a fire within, one I knew I wouldn't be able to put out anytime soon. These men were watching us with eagerness, envious of where Slater stood, anticipating his next move.

My heart continued to thrash beneath my chest as I dug my fingers deep into the cool sand beneath the surface, to numb the tingling sensation that had invaded them. I couldn't deny the intense chemistry that had sparked between us. For the first time, I was yearning for this guy, who I'd just met, to take me here on the beach, while the other stray, single men looked on. Never had I had such kinky thoughts. But knowing I would be the other men's object of desire as they watched from afar, put my excitement level into overdrive. The erotic fantasies I was experiencing were mind-blowing and so new.

I sat up and patted my towel, not hiding my eagerness of wanting him beside me. "Of course you can join me."

"Great," he said, followed by a killer smile that tickled my heart.

I watched intently as he laid his surfboard on the sand, unzipped his wetsuit, and slipped out of his sleeves, letting the arms of the suit hang freely from his waist.

I took in a subtle deep breath and subconsciously traced my lips with my tongue when I saw his well-tanned chest and his razor-sharp abs just inches from my face. He was the type of breathtakingly gorgeous a woman only sees in her dreams.

I scooched over on the towel to give him some room and again patted the space. He followed my gesture and took a seat. A spark jolted through me when his cold wetsuit touched my thigh.

"Mind if I take this off?" he asked gesturing to his suit. "It needs to dry in the sun."

"No, not all," I replied, trying to hide the elevated nervousness in my voice.

Unable to peel my eyes away, I watched intensely while he slid his perfect body out of the damp suit and laid it flat next to him.

Wearing only a pair of tight-fitting, black swimming trunks that left nothing to the imagination when it came to his bulge—which, by the way, filled his trunks nicely—he turned to face me again, putting just inches between us. As we lay face-to-face, our bodies stretched out and our heads propped up on our hands, I could feel the warmth of his breath hovering over my lips. I closed my eyes for just a second while I inhaled his masculine musk scent. Thoughts of kissing him clouded my mind and I quickly diverted them with casual conversation.

"So, what kind of name is Slater? I've never heard that name before."

"It's a nickname. My real name is Ian. I work in construction and my specialty is slate tile. A few years ago, a crew began calling me Slater and it kinda stuck. Now, everyone in the biz refers to me as Slater."

"Ahh, I see. Well, I like it. It suits you."

He paused for a moment while his eyes traced my body, stalling over my breasts before continuing to my face. "So, last week, you knew I was watching you, didn't you?" he asked in a luring voice.

I didn't shy away from his stare. "Yes, I did."

"You liked to be watched?"

Unable to ignore the heat rising between us, I began to pant, small, little breaths escaping my lips, while I curled my fingers tightly into the palms of my hands. "Apparently, I do."

His upper lip quivered and with a slow sensual movement of his tongue, he moistened it. Anticipating his touch, I held my breath, trying my best to control my noticeable elevated breathing.

"Oh, so being watched is something new to you?" he asked in a deep, seductive voice.

"You're my first," I said, followed by a playful wink.

"Hmm, I like that." He laughed.

His eyes returned to my thigh that was exposed to the sun. I moved it slightly, bending my knee a little closer to his chest. He understood my gesture and with featherlike strokes, he traced the curve of my leg with his fingertips. I let out a slight gasp as my skin sizzled from his touch, sending what I could only describe as lightning bolts throughout my entire body.

The ice had been broken. He had touched me beyond my hand. I could feel myself melting beneath the butterfly touches of his fingers as he continued to follow the contour of my body, reaching down past my knee and over my calf.

Again, he used his seductive tone. "Right now, every single guy on this beach wishes they were me. Laying here beside you, smelling your scent, and touching your soft skin. Does that turn you on? Being wanted by so many men?"

I couldn't lie. "Yes, it does," I admitted.

Our mouths drew closer, our breathing intensified. "It turns me on too. Being the envy of all these guys," he whispered.

Unable to hold back and wanting to taste him, I pulled his lips to mine and kissed him hard. Leaving no part of his mouth unexplored, I tangled my tongue with his in a deep kiss. His breath was fresh and salty from surfing. Slater took the lead and while continuing to kiss me with electrifying passion, he rolled over until I was lying on my back beneath him. My breasts were pressed firmly against his chest and his eager erection rubbed up between my legs, teasing me with its presence.

I parted my legs slightly and raised my hips toward him, while pulling him closer. I squirmed beneath him, yearning to be filled. As he continued to kiss me, pushing the back of my head deeper into the sand, he moved his hips in a wide circular motion, rubbing his erection over the outside of my bikini bottoms. I moaned with pleasure. A pleasure I had never experienced before, and I didn't want it to end.

I needed to breathe and broke away from his lips. Gasping, I gripped his shoulders while resting my chin on one of them. I scanned the beach and released a satisfying grin. We were being watched intensely by numerous men, some with their hands between their legs, stroking their hard-ons, anticipating our next move. Slater was right. They were envious of him. All were probably fantasizing about seducing me and having their way with me. What a frigging turn-on this was. Why hadn't I discovered this sooner?

While I was in awe of my newfound fetish, Slater had pulled back and, with both hands, pushed me down onto the towel. Using a firm grip, he pinned me by my shoulders while mounting me. I didn't move; instead, I embraced his leadership. He leaned in, breathing heavily, and traced the base of my neck with his warm tongue. I let out a loud gasp and closed my eyes while arching my back to meet him.

Using a stern voice, he whispered close to my lips, as I inhaled his breath, "Do you want me to take you?" While waiting for my answer, he continued to lick my neck, using long, tender strokes.

I squirmed beneath him in lust, my body unable to remain still. I didn't take long to answer. "Yes," I panted while chewing on my lower lip.

He continued to caress my neck with soft licks and kisses. I yearned for him to move his mouth down to my breasts that were itching to be touched. I arched my back again, but he ignored my desire.

"Do you want those men to watch me take you?"

Turned on by the erotic thought, I squealed, "Yes! I want them to watch. I want them to wish they were you." I didn't care that I was on a public beach. I was overpowered by the fantasy and totally out of control. Once again, the animal was out of its cage.

Slater pressed his body into mine and looked deep into my eyes before nibbling the bottom of my chin. "I want that too. I want to show them that I am the luckiest guy in the world."

His words sent shivers of excitement through me. I wanted him to take me now, but Slater had other plans. In the midst of our passion, he suddenly stopped and rolled his body off mine. Frustrated and confused, I threw him a puzzled look. "Where are you going?"

He laughed and shot me a playful wink. "Follow me," he said, holding out his hand.

CHAPTER 9

SLATER

It took all my willpower to pull myself away from Sabela. But if I hadn't, there was no doubt in my mind, we would be having sex on the beach right about now and knowing my luck, someone would more than likely report us. I figured it was better to play it safe.

Our audience was probably wondering what the hell I was doing. As soon as the heat was on, I broke away, leaving them with a lonely boner and a tired hand. I mentally sent them reassurance. *Don't worry, fellas, it's just intermission time. More to follow soon. I promise.* I was still blown away we were doing this. Discovering this turn-on with Sabela was pretty fantastic. What's really cool is that, like me, she's totally into it.

I took Sabela's hand, curling her fingers around mine. "Come with me."

She frowned in confusion. "Where are we going?"

"I'm going to have my way with you, but I can't here," I replied, with a deeper, forceful voice.

She threw me a satisfying smile and happily rose from the towel. "And where do you plan on taking me?" she asked, with such an innocence I found amusing, when I knew she couldn't wait to be the center of attention. Not only by me, but by strangers too. The thought hardened my already aching erection.

"I bet there are some secluded spots up behind these rocks someplace. And do you want to know something else?"

"What?"

"I bet you anything, our audience will follow us."

Her enticing grin told me she liked the idea. "Really? They may think we're leaving to get away from them."

"I'm a guy, I know how their minds are working. All's I need to do is glance their way and they'll understand it's okay to follow. Don't ask me how I know. I just know."

Sabela's smile grew, then she laughed. "Okay. You're the guy."

While still holding her hand, we strolled down the beach, leaving our stuff in place, and searched for an ideal spot. I gave the closest spectator a friendly smile as we walked by, letting him know we were okay with him watching us. He understood and rose to his feet to follow us, another guy soon doing the same.

After a few minutes, I saw an opening in some tall rocks and pulled Sabela in their direction. "This might be good," I said, feeling excited by the discovery.

Sabela agreed and with haste, we headed between the rocks. It was perfect. Once past the gap, we were hidden from the rest of the beach. Rock formations spanned all around us, stretching twenty feet high. The ground was sand and, to my surprise, reached back probably a good thirty feet. It was perfect for our little game.

"This is cool!" Sabela squealed, straining her neck to look up at the opening toward the sky.

I stood behind her and wrapped my arms around her waist. Resting my chin on her shoulder, I whispered in her ear, "You are so fucking hot. As soon as our guests arrive, I'm going to have my way with you."

Sabela nuzzled her head against mine. "I can't wait."

CHAPTER 10

SABELA

I couldn't believe this was happening, or that I was actually doing this. I'd just met Slater less than thirty minutes ago and I'd never wanted a guy so much as I did right now. He made me feel so sexy and alive. I was feeling incredible.

When he circled his arms around my waist, I closed my eyes and surrendered myself to his touch. I spun my body to face him and pulled him in, kissing him passionately. "God, I want you," I moaned between breaths.

He responded by kissing me with greater force, thrusting his tongue into my mouth. I clung to him, not wanting to let go, devouring his taste and scent.

His muscular hands moved down to my ass, cupping my cheeks as he squeezed them hard and dug into my flesh with his nails. I moved my hips in a circular motion, grinding my body against his as I felt the dampness between my legs intensify.

A scuffle of feet caught my attention and while still locked in a kiss, I opened one eye and looked over his shoulder. Fifteen feet away, two men stood about ten feet apart. A rush of excitement raced through me and I pinched Slater's shoulder. He stopped and pulled himself away from my lips. He turned in the men's direction and threw them a welcoming smile. The men, understanding it was okay to be there, smiled back.

Slater whispered in my ear, "Let the show begin," followed by a mischievous grin.

I didn't acknowledge the guys before us. Not yet. Just being aware of their presence ignited an even greater desire to be taken by Slater. Anticipating that actual moment sent my head into a tailspin, and I didn't know how long I could hold out before I would scream, *"Take me now!"*

While lost in my erotic thoughts, Slater surprised me when he broke loose of our hold. "I want these men to appreciate your beauty as much as I do," he murmured. With one hand, he traced the contour of my face, stopping at my chin. He lifted it slightly with his thumb and forefinger and gave me a gentle kiss. "I want them to envision touching you, when I'm touching you. Do you like that idea?"

"Yes," was all I could manage to say, my eyes closed and my body trembling with lust.

I stood before him, my arms hanging freely at my sides. I was under his spell, and the object of desire for three men. The rush I was experiencing was incredible. With each movement of Slater's hand, my breathing intensified until my chest was heaving with repetitive short pants.

To be sure the other men had a clear view of him caressing every inch of my body, Slater put space between us. I closed my eyes and raised my head slightly as I felt the roughness of his hand move down to my bikini top. With tender touches, he traced the V of the material between my breasts, reaching inside for just a moment and giving my nipple a sharp pinch. I gasped and released a loud moan of pleasure. My nipples, now hard and standing to attention, peeked through the soft material. Slater leaned down and gave my left one a slight nip with his teeth, sending another wave of passionate heat through me.

Using both hands, he continued to knead my breasts while working his way down to my stomach with his moist tongue and soft lips. Slater fell to his knees and I released another gasp as I felt the warmth of his tongue glide across my abs and into my belly button. Bracing myself, I clenched handfuls of his hair in my fists while pulling him closer. I threw my head back and pushed out my chest, slightly parting my legs as I anticipated his touch.

With the glide of his tongue, he crested the top of my bikini bottoms. The heat of his breath was within inches of my saturated core, which was now beginning to pulsate as his mouth inched closer. His hands left my breasts and moved to my thighs.

"Spread your legs further. I want our friends to enjoy what I'm seeing."

I obeyed and pushed my feet apart in the sand. At the mention of the other men, I took my first glance at where they were sitting and made eye contact with one. Both sat naked in the sand, stroking their erect shafts with rapid movements of the wrists. I threw the strangers a subtle smile before throwing back my head at the feel of Slater's tongue teasing my most sensual spot.

He had his head buried between my legs, his hot breath brushing at the lips of my hungry core. I held my breasts, pushing them closer together as I kneaded each one deeply with my palms, and gave my nipples the occasional squeeze. I took another sneak-peek at our audience, whose eyes were glued to the live sex show before them. When my eyes met with the guy sitting on the left, I traced my lips with my tongue and threw him a flirty smile, before tossing my head back into a heated frenzy of ecstasy as Slater gently drew my bikini bottoms away from my skin and slid two of his fingers inside me. My body jolted from the sudden waves of electrifying sensations I was experiencing.

As Slater worked his magic with his fingers, the cool air brushing across my crotch gave me a sense of freedom. I thrust my hips toward him and began gyrating over his hand, riding his fingers deeper inside me. A loud whimper of pleasure escaped when I felt the heat of his breath brush the lips of my throbbing core. I released another deep moan as the tip of his tongue entered me. I didn't know how much longer I could last. Caught in the moment, not having a care in the world, I became louder. I wanted Slater inside of me. He knew I was ready for him but insisted on torturing me some more. With my juices now plentiful to taste, he teased me with his fingers, using a fast-rhythmic pace while exploring the outside with sensual licks.

I was out of control and ready to explode as each stroke of his tongue drew me closer to the edge of an orgasm. My body trembled. I ached to have him inside of me. After a few more minutes of intensifying teasing licks, he finally whispered in a heated breath, "Are you ready for me?"

"Yes!" I squealed while grinding my hips in front of his face.

"Do you want these men to watch me enter you and fantasize about being inside of you?"

"Oh god, yes!" I pleaded.

Removing his fingers, he slowly peeled my bikini bottoms down my legs while kissing my thighs. When they were around my feet, I eagerly stepped out of them.

Slater gave my behind a hard slap. I winced from the sudden sting while, at the same time, I found myself turned on by his leadership and force. "Turn around. I want them to see your beautiful behind."

I didn't hesitate and spun around.

"Bend over," he commanded.

Again, I obeyed while cupping my breasts and giving them a hard squeeze.

Slater gave my cheek another smack. "God, you're perfect." He glanced at the men and threw them a smile before he buried his face between my cheeks. I wriggled my body while bending at the hips and grinding against his face. Again, he smacked me and with force, he pushed on my inner thighs with his palms. "Spread your legs wide, so our friends can see my me slide in and out of you."

With a quick movement of his body, Slater peeled off his trunks. I looked over my shoulder and focused my eyes on his hard, throbbing erection, now being stroked by his hand as he glided the tip over the soft skin of my behind.

"Do you want it?" he said between short breaths.

"Yes," I begged.

"Spread your cheeks for me, so our audience can see me enter you," Slater commanded.

Using both hands, I reached around and grabbed my butt cheeks, pulling them as far apart as I could. The cool air whispered up inside of me. I leaned farther forward, preparing myself to take him. I didn't have to wait long. With one quick thrust, Slater plunged deep inside of me. My body tensed up with his invasion as I released a loud, satisfying moan. God, he felt good.

Slater held my hips tight, digging his nails into my flesh, using them for balance as he delved deeper into my core with every thrust. Each one was followed by a satisfactory grunt. I tilted my hips higher, wanting to feel every inch of his length fill my inner walls. He didn't disappoint. As his pace quickened, I kneaded my breasts harder, grasping them in the palms of my hands, pinching my nipples with the tips of my fingers.

Thoughts of the two men watching entered my head. With every thrust of Slater's shaft, I knew they were fantasying about being inside of me. What a rush! I glanced in their direction and threw them a devious smile. One of them smiled back while stroking his prominent erection with speed. I locked my eyes on his and licked my lips before raising one of my breasts up to my mouth and slowly circled my nipple with soft, gentle teases of my tongue.

Slater's thrusts became quicker and harder. I met his speed with my hips, grinding myself deep across his thighs. His breathing intensified, his groans of pleasure becoming louder. I knew, at any moment, he would be releasing his hot come into me.

"Do you like that?" Slater grunted between pants.

Squeezing my eyes closed, I squealed, "Yes!" As my body began to tense up with signs of an explosive orgasm approaching. Slater could no longer hold back and with one final, forceful thrust, he plunged deeper and allowed his juices to flow, followed by loud moans of exuberant pleasure. I held my breasts harder as I shook my head vigorously from side to side. Each sharp jolt of his thrusts was bringing me closer to the edge.

"Don't stop!" I panted while reaching around and squeezing the cheeks of his behind, trying desperately to pull him deeper inside of me.

Knowing I was on the brink of an orgasm, he sped up his rhythm. "Come on, baby. Let these men see you come," Slater moaned in my ear.

His reminder that we were being watched put me over the edge and I instantly let out a loud gratifying scream as my orgasm riveted through my entire body. I pulled Slater closer, as our bodies jerked repeatedly, draining every drop of orgasmic juice.

For a few moments after, with our hearts still pounding, we both were lifeless, like ragdolls, our eyes closed, our bodies limp and drenched with sweat. Once his heart rate was back to normal, Slater raised his head and gave it a good shake. "Wow!"

I laughed at his satisfactory cry. "Wow is right. Damn, what just happened?" I said while shifting my body.

Slater slowly pulled himself out of me, allowing a few drips of juices to trickle down my legs. I stood up straight and stretched my back. Moans from the other men caught our attention. We both turned and glanced in their direction, just in time to see them cleaning themselves off between their legs with their shorts.

"Looks like everyone will be leaving happy." Slater chuckled before sending them a satisfying smile. The men reciprocated with grins of their own. No words were spoken but they knew it was time to leave. Before putting on their now damp shorts, they threw me a smile. Now wrapped in Slater's arms, I smiled back while waiting for them to exit.

Standing behind me, his arms crossed over my chest, Slater nuzzled his face in the crook of my neck while peppering it with gentle kisses. "Damn, girl. You were hot."

"You weren't so bad yourself." I laughed at his comment. "You got me all hot and bothered." I strained my neck to look up at him. "It's all your fault. I've never acted this way before," I said, while giving a mocking look of innocence. "What have you done to me?"

"I think being watched had a lot to do with it," Slater said, then playfully pinched my boob.

Still circled in his arms, I spun my body around and snaked my arms around his waist before kissing him hard on the lips. "That was insane. I've never been so friggin' turned on in my whole life. I can't believe what we just did, and I'm still trying to wrap my head around it."

Slater nuzzled my nose with his. "You know, I've had plenty of sex in my days, but never in front of an audience. That was pretty wild." He laughed. "Looks like they had a good time too. Did you see the smiles on their faces when they left?"

I rested my head on Slater's sweaty chest while he gently massaged my shoulder. "I wonder if it was the first time for those guys too? Do you think they've watched other couples have sex before? Or did we just blow their minds?" I laughed.

Slater kissed the top of my head. "Oh, I'd like to think we blew their minds. But we can ask them next time."

I looked up before giving him a friendly slap on the chest. "Slater! What do you mean, next time? And I don't want to talk to them. In fact, I don't want to know anything about them."

He laughed at the ground rules I was making over our newfound fetish.

"I was joking. I don't want to talk to them either. Being anonymous is part of the game, right? But you know as well as I do, this won't be the last time we'll allow ourselves to be watched."

I shrugged my shoulders. "I don't know. It's not like we planned this. I had no idea this was going to happen." I smiled. "But I do like the idea that I'm going to see you again."

Slater smiled back and gave my body a hard squeeze. "Sabela, you've swept me off my feet. I plan on seeing you for a long time. Now come on, we should get back to our stuff."

Knowing I wasn't just a one-time fling comforted me. "Okay," I said with a gloating smile.

CHAPTER 11

SLATER

*W*hile walking back to our spot on the beach, I noticed our companions had left. I chuckled, knowing the events of the day would stick with them for a long time. I held Sabela's hand tight. She was right, neither one of us had planned it, but damn, we were like friggin' animals out of control. Talk about self-discovery—I never knew I had such a wild side.

When we reached the towel, and found everything in place, Sabela took a seat and reached for her shorts.

"Leaving already?" I asked.

"In a bit. I need to go home and take a shower. I have sand in places I shouldn't," she said, followed by a cute giggle.

I joined her on the towel, admiring the glow of satisfaction she radiated. If I sat here long enough, I knew I'd be all over her again. "Can I take you out for dinner tonight?" I placed my hand on her thigh. It tingled from the softness of her skin. "Now that we've gotten the 'I want to fuck your brains out' part over with, I'd like to get to know you," I said, throwing her a devious smile. "I know nothing about you, except that you like to be watched while getting fucked by a guy you just met on the beach."

She threw her head back, laughing at my humorous comment. "Hey, I don't make a habit of it. I told you that you were my first." She gave my hand a gentle squeeze. "I'd like to get to know you too. Dinner sounds great."

"Well, you're going to have tell me where there's a good place to eat. I'm new to this area and don't know of any decent restaurants."

Sabela pondered for a minute. "There's a good restaurant right on Pacific Coast Highway, it's called The Ocean Front Grill. We can meet there, if you'd like?"

"Sounds good to me. I'll go home and shower too, and meet you there at seven. How would that be?"

"I'd love it," she replied with a beautiful, innocent smile, which I found ironic after what we had just done.

I released a cocky laugh. "This is too funny."

"What is?" Sabela asked, looking puzzled.

"We made out on the beach, snuck off to some isolated spot, allowed strangers to watch us fuck while we got totally turned on, and now we're planning our first date. I think we're doing this backwards."

Sabela joined me in my laugh while nuzzling her body close to mine. "Well, I guess people have been doing it wrong all this time."

CHAPTER 12

SABELA

*I*t was hard to pull myself away from Slater. Never in my wildest dreams did I think I would allow strangers to watch me get laid. Funny thing is, Slater was a stranger too. but ironically, he didn't feel like one. I felt liberated, wild, and free, and it felt friggin' awesome. Again, I asked myself, why hadn't I discovered this sooner?

Reluctantly, I got dressed, exchanged phone numbers with Slater, and gathered my things. I rolled up my towel and tucked it under my arm.

Now dressed in his wetsuit, Slater embraced me and pulled me in closer. I felt the heat rising between us again as I began to melt beneath the tender touch of his lips pressed against mine. I met his kiss, exploring his mouth with my tongue. After a few seconds, I pulled myself away and giggled. Fighting my desires, I used my hand as a shield and pressed my hand against his chest. "Okay, I gotta go."

Slater grabbed me again and playfully touched his nose with mine. "I know. I'm just having a hard time letting you go. I'll see you tonight, okay?"

I gave him a warm smile before releasing his hold on me. "I can't wait," I said, and kissed him one last time before heading home.

I didn't walk across the beach, I skipped while my heart beat a joyful tune. I couldn't hide the smile that blanketed my face. Halfway across the beach, I turned to see Slater still standing where I had left him, his smile matching mine, and gave him a final wave. I couldn't wait for our first date tonight. Slater was right, we were doing it backwards. I laughed at the thought but in a way, it made it easier. Most first dates are ruined by the invasion of nervous energy from spending most of the night wondering if they were going to end up in bed together. Slater and I had already surpassed that hurdle. Tonight, nothing could ruin it.

Ten minutes later, I was back in my duplex, still stunned by the afternoon events. *Wow* was all that kept coming to mind. Sometimes I'd say it out loud. Funny thing was, I couldn't imagine playing this game with any other guy. He loved it as much as I did and the chemistry between us was explosive. There was no doubt, I had already fallen hard for him. I wasn't only anticipating having sex with him again, I was also wondering who would be watching us next.

Devious thoughts continued to cloud my mind while I stepped into the shower and let the spray of warm water stream down my body. I closed my eyes and embraced myself, reflecting back to the beach. Thoughts of being wrapped in Slater's arms comforted me. I couldn't help but smile. I hadn't felt this content in a long time and couldn't wait to see him again.

After stepping out of the shower, I checked the clock above the mirror and saw it was only five, giving me two hours to kill before our date. The next thirty minutes were spent deciding what to wear. The nights were still warm so I chose a white flared mini summer dress with thin shoulder spaghetti straps. I found my cutest white, lace thong and seamless sheer bra, allowing the dress to hug my body better.

By the time I had gotten dressed, dried my hair, and applied my makeup, it was already quarter after six. I would have to leave in the next twenty minutes to make it on time. I spent the next ten minutes trying to find a matching pair of shoes in the pile of disarray on my closet floor. With one white sandal in my hand, I began tossing shoes over my shoulder, trying to find its match. I finally found it, buried at the bottom of the pile. "There you are," I said out loud, feeling relieved my search was over.

I hastily grabbed a light white sweater, leaving the coat hanger swinging as I pulled it free, and scurried to the living room to put on my sandals. I glanced at the clock on the wall and saw it was time to leave. I located my phone on the bathroom counter and my purse on the floor by the couch. It took me another couple of minutes to find my car keys at the bottom of my purse. With them finally in my hand, I tossed my phone in my purse, grabbed my sweater from the couch, and headed out the door.

Two minutes later, I was seated comfortably in my car with the seat belt buckled and the radio tuned to classic rock. After rechecking I had everything, I backed out of my parking space and pulled out onto Pacific Coast Highway, in the direction of the restaurant.

Five minutes into the drive, while singing along to the loud songs blasting from the radio, flashing red and blue lights caught my attention in the rearview mirror. "What? I wasn't speeding," I said loudly as I slowly maneuvered my car to the side of the road and left the motor running in idle.

Patiently, I waited, peering in my rearview mirror and wondering why I had been pulled me over. A few seconds later, I saw a heavyset officer step out of the patrol car and cautiously approach my vehicle on the passenger side while talking into his handheld radio. I was curious what he was saying. I pushed the button on the door to roll down the passenger side window and waited with sweaty palms and elevated nerves, counting every one of his footsteps until he reached my car.

I was stunned to see his hand lightly positioned over his gun, hanging from his hip. Did I look like a threat? Afraid to move, I froze in my seat and waited for the officer to speak first. With his hand still shadowing his weapon, he lowered his head and peered through my window. He spoke in a stern voice. "Ma'am, I need you to raise your hands and step out of the vehicle."

"What?" I replied shrilly, placing my hands away from the steering wheel and in front of me.

After giving me his orders, the officer marched around the back of my car and opened the driver's side door. "Please step out of the vehicle and do not make any sudden moves."

I could feel a knot beginning to form in my throat. I swallowed hard, trying to dislodge it, but failed. This didn't feel like a routine traffic stop. He hadn't even asked me for my driver's license or registration, and the way his hand didn't leave his side scared the crap out of me.

Moving like a tortoise, afraid of jerking my body in any way that may be considered a sudden move, I carefully eased myself out of the car. The second my feet touched the ground and I was standing straight, the officer reached for his handcuffs and spun me around while holding both my hands behind my back. His grip was strong.

"What is going on?" I protested while straining my neck to look at him.

I felt the cold metal of the cuffs against my skin as they were snapped into place. With another forceful push, he turned my head away, kicked the insides of my ankles to spread my feet, and patted down my body from head to toe while still holding the cuffs in place.

Feeling violated and scared, my body trembled with fear. Tears flooded my eyes while I pleaded with the officer, "What is going on, officer? I haven't done anything wrong."

The cop grabbed my shoulder and jerked my body away from the car while still holding onto my cuffed hands, and proceeded to lead me to the patrol car. "The vehicle you are driving has been reported as stolen. I'm taking you in and booking you for grand theft auto."

I tried to turn my head in protest, but the officer had a good grip on my neck. "What!" I shrieked. "There has to be some sort of mistake! It was given to me."

That's when it occurred to me Davin did this. He'd reported the car stolen. *Oh, my god! How could he do this? Why would he do this? This can't be happening.*

I tried to reason with the cop. "Look, officer. I know who did this. It was my ex-boyfriend. He gave me the car." The cop listened but said nothing, so I pleaded some more. "He's mad because I wouldn't move to Texas with him. Surely, we can call him or something, and sort this out?"

The cop continued to lead me to the patrol car. "I'm not here to iron out your domestic disputes. That's something you'll have to take up with the judge." He paused at the back of the patrol car and opened the door. "Now, come on. Get in."

Tears were now gushing down my face as he lowered my head and settled me into the car. I'd never been to jail before. I was petrified. How could Davin do this? Then I remembered Slater. Oh, my god! What about Slater? He's going to think I stood him up. If that wasn't bad enough, it suddenly occurred to me it was the weekend, which meant I wouldn't be able to see a judge until Monday and that's only if they gave me a hearing. I could be stuck in jail for weeks. I had to get to a phone as soon as possible and call Davin. I needed to talk some sense into him. I was horrified when I realized Davin was the only person who could get me out of jail. I wondered what it was going to cost me? Davin said on the phone, he always got what he wanted.

CHAPTER 13

SLATER

I couldn't wait to see Sabela again. The afternoon at the beach had been wild. After saying goodbye to her, which was hard to do, I did some more surfing and managed to catch a couple of sets before heading home.

For the entire afternoon, images of Sabela never left my mind. I wanted to call her so many times, just to let her know I was missing her. Then it occurred to me I should have offered to pick her up. What kind of a gentleman was I, letting her drive herself to the restaurant? Damn it! I lost some brownie points on that one. *I know, I'll make it up to her by bringing her some flowers.*

At home, I took a long shower. Of course, I masturbated while thinking back to the beach and came good. After finding a clean pair of jeans and a white shirt, I splashed on some cologne, brushed my hair, and put on my loafers before heading out to my truck to bring my surfboard inside and put it on the deck.

Again, I glanced at my phone, checking to see if she had called. She hadn't, and I refrained from calling her. I think I was afraid she wasn't going to show up and I needed reassurance she would be there. I shook my head at my silliness and placed my phone in my back pocket. Of course, she'd be there. Why wouldn't she be?

I checked my room one last time to make sure I had everything and decided to leave earlier so I could pick up the flowers.

Twenty minutes later, I arrived at the restaurant with a dozen red roses in hand and fifteen minutes early for our date. The place looked busy. We hadn't made reservations and I hoped there wouldn't be a problem getting a table.

I checked my hair one more time in the rearview mirror. It looked flat from being washed and I gave my head a good shake. That did the trick. Satisfied, I grabbed the roses laying on the passenger seat and stepped out of the truck. The cool breeze felt good. I stood for a moment to enjoy it and gazed out at the magnificent view of the ocean before heading into the restaurant.

I was greeted by a cute little blonde with menus in hand. "Table for one?" she asked.

"Actually no. I'm meeting someone here. It'll be for two."

"Okay, right this way," the hostess replied with a courteous smile.

She led me to a quiet table tucked away in the corner, decorated with a single white carnation in a glass vase. "Here you go. Your waiter will be right with you," she tells me, while placing two menus on the edge of the table.

I pulled out one of the wooden chairs. "Thanks," I replied, taking a seat and laying the roses down on the table.

Once alone, I scanned the restaurant. Sabela had good taste. It was a cozy place, with additional outside seating on a deck that overlooked the ocean. Old black-and-white pictures of fishermen and their boats covered the walls. Nautical items consisting of fish nets, buoys, and mounted fish added to the décor.

A few minutes later, a tall blond waiter approached my table. I knew right away he was a fellow surfer. Probably a waiter by night who spent all his days trying to catch the big one. I knew the feeling too well. He looked to be in his early twenties. "Hi, I'm

Aaron and I'll be your waiter this evening." He glanced down at the two menus sitting on the table. "It looks like you're waiting for someone. Can I get you something to drink?"

"Yeah, that would be great. I'll take a rum and Coke."

"Sure, man. I'll be right back."

While waiting for my drink to arrive, I decided to scan the menu. The selection was good. They had a huge variety of seafood and a small selection of steaks and chicken for the non-seafood lovers. Being a huge seafood fan, I could see the choice was going to be difficult.

A few minutes later, the waiter arrived with my drink. "Here you go," he said, placing the glass on the table.

I reached for the drink and gave it a quick stir with the small red straws. "Thanks."

"You're welcome. If you need anything else before your guest arrives, let me know," the waiter informed me before heading to the table behind me with a newly seated couple.

Once he left, I laid the red straws on the napkin and took a large gulp of the drink. It produced instant gratification and drowned any nerves I had been feeling. I looked at my watch and saw it was five minutes after seven. Sabela was late. I glanced down the row of tables, in the hopes of seeing her, but to no avail. I had no idea if she was a prompt person like myself. I wasn't too worried. I knew, living by the beach, traffic was always a factor that often interfered with our schedules.

Thinking she may call to let me know she was running late, I reached into to my back pocket and pulled out my phone. After seeing there was no missed calls or texts from her I placed it on the table.

By seven thirty, I was beginning to worry. The waiter had checked back and brought me another drink, which I'd already drank half of, and there was still no sign of Sabela. My first thought was she was standing me up, but that didn't make any sense. I clearly felt her enthusiasm when I asked her to dinner tonight. The smile she beamed at me was genuine.

I glanced at my phone again and decided to call her but it went straight to voicemail. Hearing her voice brought a smile to my face. I waited for the beep. "Hey, Sabela, it's Slater. I'm at the restaurant. Just wondering where you are. It's seven thirty, I'm getting hungry." I chuckled. "Call me. Bye." I ended the call, wondering if maybe she was in a dead zone or if her phone had died.

The waiter returned and glanced at the flowers. "First date?" he asked.

I smirked, thinking of my first encounter with Sabela. "Kind of."

"Ahh, no worries, man. I'm sure she'll show up. Can I get you another drink?"

"No, I'm good, thanks," I answered, then proceeded to take another large gulp of the one I had.

For the next fifteen minutes, I found myself constantly checking my phone, making sure it was still working and that the volume was turned up high. It was. Why hadn't she called? I was baffled. Then I had a horrific thought. *Maybe she's been in an accident.* I panicked, grabbed my phone, and tried calling her again, only to get her voicemail one more time. The more I thought about it, the more I suspected something had happened, because nothing else made sense. Damn it! Why didn't I pick her up?

I didn't believe Sabela stood me up. She didn't seem the type. My gut was telling me something was wrong. God, I wish she'd answer her damn phone.

With no way of getting a hold of her or even knowing where she lived—another reason why I should have picked her up—I flagged down the waiter and asked for my check.

He approached my table with a long face, obviously trying to show me some compassion. "Sorry, man. But there's plenty of other fish in the sea."

Scowling, I shot him a piercing stare and slammed some dollars down on the table. "No, there's not." Irritated by his stupid comment, I grabbed the flowers, still intending to give them to her, and stood from the table. After retrieving my phone and checking it one more time. I slid it into my back pocket while telling the waiter to keep the change, and hastily left the restaurant.

When I was finally in the solitude of my truck, I leaned back and closed my eyes. In my mind, I re-lived every moment of the glorious afternoon I had spent with Sabela, trying to see if I had missed anything where I may have upset her in any way. But there wasn't. If anything, I sensed when it was time for her to leave, she had a hard time pulling herself away, just like I did. I tried calling her again with no luck and threw the phone down on the passenger seat next to the roses.

I shook my head in despair and before firing up the truck, I glanced around the parking lot one last time, in the hopes of seeing her. I didn't, and a wave of disappointment washed over me.

Realizing there was nothing I could do but head home and wait for her to call me had me beating myself up one more time for not picking her up. I hated this feeling of being a sitting duck. I needed to know why she didn't show up. Thoughts that she may never call crossed my mind, but I quickly shook them off, believing she'd never do that. The connection we had was too strong. I felt it. I know I did.

It was now eight fifteen. Reluctantly, and confused, I pulled out of the parking lot and headed home with no idea what had happened to Sabela.

CHAPTER 14

SABELA

Sitting in the back of the patrol car, I became a hysterical mess. Tears were streaming down my face and my body was trembling with fear at the thought of going to jail.

I watched while the cop went to my car and retrieved my purse. A few minutes later, he returned and emptied the contents onto the hood of the patrol car. While holding my driver's license, he mumbled some cop jargon into his radio. After putting all my belongings back into my purse, he returned to the driver's seat and continued to fill out some paperwork.

"Officer, you have to believe me. I didn't steal that car," I cried out while sobbing.

He showed no compassion. "Ma'am, I've already told you that you have to take it up with the judge. Now, I'd appreciate it if you would remain quiet. We will be on our way shortly."

I cowered in my seat, feeling like I was living a nightmare. This couldn't be happening to me. But it was and there was nothing I could do. I couldn't believe Davin had done this to me, and why? I knew he was upset with me for not going to Texas, but why have me arrested? Was this supposed to change my mind? His actions weren't making any sense.

Within a few minutes, a tow truck appeared. I watched as they hooked up my car and towed it away. Once my car was in custody, the cop started up the patrol car and pulled away from the curb.

Feeling ashamed to be sitting in a cop car, handcuffed, tears continued to mask my face as I held my head low away from the window, shielding it from any passing cars all the way to the county jail.

When we arrived, the cop kept me in handcuffs as I was led through three heavy iron gates, all of which automatically closed with a loud heavy *bang* behind us. My ears shuddered from the sound. No words were said. I was shuffled like a piece of cattle until I was handed an orange jumpsuit. My handcuffs were finally removed when they took my photo and fingerprints. Before putting on the jumpsuit, I was ordered to disrobe and go stand against a cold concrete wall.

Afraid to make any sudden moves, I did as I was told and while my body shivered, I waited for the next command. A large mean-looking woman that could probably beat up ten of me, gave me the onceover, scanning my body from head to toe with her shady eyes. With her stale breath within inches of my face, she ordered me to turn around and spread my legs.

"Why?" I asked through my continued sobs.

"No questions. Do as I say, and we'll be through this in no time."

I didn't argue and did as I was told. Feeling violated, I spread my legs and felt my body cringe as I allowed this beast of a woman to inspect every vortex of my body with her gloved hands. I had never felt so humiliated or scared in my entire life.

After what seemed like hours, the guard finally backed away, handed me some white cotton underwear from a box, and told me to get dressed in the jumpsuit. I couldn't move fast enough and hastily covered my body with the not-so-flattering wardrobe.

Feeling somewhat human again, I was led through a wide corridor of holding tanks. There must have been at least ten of them, all filled to their capacity with female inmates.

I avoided eye contact with the women, keeping my eyes glued to the floor for most of the time as I walked by. Many peered through the bars, while whistling and wetting their lips with their tongues. It was obvious some were prostitutes from the way they were dressed in their short tight mini dresses, high heels, and heavy makeup. The stench of alcohol was overpowering. It occurred to me that no one in those cells were wearing the ugly orange jumpsuits. Did that mean I was going to be here longer, or hadn't they gone through the awful experience I had just endured?

At the end of the hallway, the guard came to an abrupt stop and faced the last holding tank. Magically, the iron gates slid open. "Go on in," she ordered without looking my way.

"When will I be able to make a phone call?" I asked, my voice still trembling.

"You'll get your turn. Now come on, I don't have all day."

I turned and faced the cell. About a dozen women of many different nationalities, and all dressed in the jumpsuits, stared my way. I hung my head low, shadowing my eyes, and shuffled my way in. The metal gates quickly closed behind me, and again I shuddered from the loud *bang*. I quickly scanned the ten-by-ten cell and spotted an isolated corner at the end of the bench, and quickly claimed it.

The woman next to me reeked of alcohol and was unable to hold up her head. She turned toward me and coughed. I faced the other way, holding my breath. "Whatcha in here for, darlin'?" she slurred.

I answered in a defensive voice, "They said I stole a car. But it's all a mistake."

"It always is, darlin'. They say I'm drunk. Look at me. Do I look drunk to you?"

I didn't answer. Instead, I shifted my body a few inches further away from her and lowered my head into my hands. I couldn't believe this was happening. Does Davin even realize what he's putting me through? How could he do this?

My thoughts then switched to Slater. I had no idea what time it was, but knew it was well past seven. He probably left, thinking I had stood him up. *Oh, Slater, I'm so sorry, but there's no way for me to call you. I wish you could help me get out of this awful mess. You're the first person I'm going to call once I get out of this forsaken hellhole. In the meantime, I can't wait to have a few choice words with Davin. Dammit! When do I get to make my phone call?*

CHAPTER 15

SABELA

I don't know how many hours they kept me in that cell but it felt like an eternity. Two of the women approached me while I was trying to keep to myself and mind my own business. One asked what I was in for, then laughed liked a hyena when I told her and wished me luck. The other, a colored heavyset woman, combed my hair with her fingers and told me if I needed a friend during my stay, to come hunt her down. I shook my head vigorously while my body cringed beneath her touch. When she was finally called by the guards and taken away, my body relaxed and I let out a huge sigh of relief.

A few hours later, the same guard approached the cell and called my name. I quickly stood to attention and made way to the entrance. "Follow me," she said in a cold voice with no heart.

She led me through corridors of smaller cells, which echoed with inmates whistling and laughing. I looked straight ahead. I didn't want to know any of these women. Finally, she came to a stop and a cell on our right opened. "In you go," she said, using the same heartless tone.

I nodded and shuffled in. A frail, young blonde woman was curled up in the corner of the lower bunk, sobbing with her head buried in her knees. I let her be and climbed up to the top bed, thankful to be in a quieter place. "Do you know when I'll be able to make a phone call?" I asked the guard before she locked me up like an animal.

She gave me a cold stare that made me cringe and simply said, "Soon," before walking away.

I threw my head down in frustration on the flat pillow of the bunk, curled my body, and added to the sobbing sounds my cellmate was making below with my own tears until I drifted off to sleep.

I don't know how long I had been sleeping, but we were rudely awakened by a loud female voice. "Rise and shine, ladies. Time to get up and eat breakfast."

I stretched out long, my back hurting from the poor excuse of a mattress that had no padding. I rubbed where it hurt and lowered myself off the bed on to the floor. I glanced at the blonde woman, who was no longer crying.

"Hi," I said softly.

She nodded in response.

"What time is it?" I asked the guard.

"Five a.m. Now, come on. We don't have all day."

Outside the cell, she had us stand in line with at least a hundred other inmates, and led us into a large dining hall filled with metal table and benches. We were ordered to grab a blue plastic tray and wait in line for our food. I kept to myself and stuck close to my cellmate, who seemed harmless.

While in line, I asked if she was okay, noticing her eyes were red and swollen from her tears last night. I could tell she appreciated my concerned words and knew I wasn't going to harm her. She gave me a silent nod followed by a subtle smile.

We stayed together and sat at the same table, along with eight other women whose stares I avoided after giving a formal, shy "Hi" to the table.

The blonde and I exchanged our stories. Her name was Julie and she was twenty-five. I was surprised she was in for assault and battery against her boyfriend. She was so tiny and frail and probably couldn't hurt a fly, but I believed her when she swore it was self-defense.

After eating the paste, they called oatmeal, and the dry cardboard they said was toast, one of the guards announced in a loud voice, "Anyone that needs to make a phone call, stand up and step away from the table."

Julie and I stood, along with half the room. "God, this is going to take hours," I mumbled under my breath.

We were led in single file out of the big hall into a corridor lined with a dozen payphones. We were told to stay in line and wait for the next available phone. The guard informed us each call would be limited to five minutes. When the time was up, the phone would automatically shut off.

I was glad Davin's mom had insisted he have a landline at his apartment. Her words were, *"You can't always relay on those damn cell phones."* If she hadn't, there would have been no way I could call Davin collect. The number was easy to remember too. When he had given it to me, I laughed because I noticed the last four numbers spelled out *DICK*. How appropriate that is now. God, I can't wait to give him a piece of my mind for putting me through this. What a fucking asshole!

As I stood in line, a large tattooed woman, with skin the color of mocha, turned to face me and winked. "Hi, beautiful."

My heart pounded beneath my chest while I hugged my body to make a shield. "Hi," I mumbled while looking down at the ground, hoping she wouldn't spark up a conversation.

"Who you calling? Your daddy?" She laughed with noticeable sarcasm.

Not wanting to engage in any kind of chitchat with her, I simply said, "No."

She laughed again, but louder. "Daddy's little girl has been naughty. What did you do, Buttercup?"

Feeling intimidated, I shifted on my feet and held my body tighter. In the nicest voice possible, I answered, hoping I wouldn't piss her off. "I really don't want to talk about it."

She raised her hands and cracked another laugh. "Okay, honey. Just trying to kill some time while we stand here waiting. No need to get hissy on me. I'm sure Daddy will help you."

To my relief, she turned away and began talking to the tiny oriental girl in front of her.

After an immense length of time, I was finally next in line. I waited anxiously for the next phone to become available, wishing everyone would hurry up. A few minutes later, I spotted a girl hang up the phone at the end of the corridor and immediately rushed over to it.

My hands shook as I picked up the phone and gave the operator Davin's number and my name. It was still early. *He shouldn't have left for classes yet*, I told myself. It rang three times. "Come on, Davin. Pick up the damn phone," I whispered with a clenched fist held up to my mouth.

On the fourth ring, I heard his voice. "Hello."

"This is the operator. I have a collect call from a Sabela Hutchinson. Will you accept the charge?"

I heard Davin chuckle and could picture the smirk smeared across his face. "Sure," he replied.

The operator went on to lay out the rules of the phone call and to remind us the call was being monitored and would be disconnected if the rules were not followed. She ended by saying, "Go ahead, Hutchinson, you're connected."

I didn't wait for Davin to speak. "How could you do this to me? I'm in jail, Davin. You have to get me out of here! I didn't steal your fucking car. You *gave* it to me," I snarled down the phone, feeling my fury towards him rise.

He showed no compassion and only laughed louder. "I told you, I always get what I want, Sabela. I miss you and you belong with me."

"What is that supposed to mean? How is me being in jail getting what you want?"

"Well, think about it. The only person that can get you out is me. Right?"

What was he up to? "I guess," I answered, knowing he was right but didn't want to admit it.

"Well, in order for that to happen, you're going to have to do what I ask."

It suddenly occurred to me what he was doing. My blood began to boil, infuriated he would do such a thing. "Are you *blackmailing* me?" I asked in a harsh tone.

"You can look at it however you want. I just want you to come to Texas. I asked you nicely before and now it's come to this. It doesn't have to be this way, Sabela. You had to be difficult. Say you'll come to Texas and I'll drop all charges. I'll tell them it was a misunderstanding. It's quite simple, really."

"I can't believe you're doing this. It's so wrong, Davin." I closed my eyes, knowing I had no other choice and the clock was ticking on our call. With reluctance, I forced myself to speak. "Fine! I'll come to Texas."

"See that wasn't so, hard, was it?" Davin snickered on the other end.

I ignored his question. "You got what you want. Now just get me out of here."

"You'd better be on a plane within a week, Sabela. I mean it, and..."

Before he could finish, our phone call was cut off. I wondered what else he was going to say? Would he do as he had promised and get me out of here? I had no way of knowing. I hung up the phone with the uncomfortable feeling of my fate being in Davin's hands.

I had promised him I would go to Texas. What would he do if I didn't?

CHAPTER 16

SLATER

For the past three days, I must have tried calling Sabela at least a dozen times. Every time, it went straight to her voicemail. I've given up and my heart is shattered. I just didn't get it. I honestly thought she was into me as much as I was into her. I guess I was wrong. I mean, when I thought about it, I knew absolutely nothing about her. Not even her last name. Maybe this was her thing. For all I know, she likes to visit the beach frequently and meet strange men for a one-time stand.

I'd gone to the beach every morning since Saturday in the hopes of seeing her, but with no luck. I even checked the police reports for accidents and nothing had been reported. Maybe her phone was stolen. It just didn't add up. My gut was telling me something was wrong. All's I could do was wait for her to call me. If she doesn't, then I know I've been fooled. I just hope that's not the case.

I moped around work today, keeping to myself. Everyone knew something was up. I was usually the jokester of the crew, keeping the guys in a good mood. Drew even pulled me aside and asked me if everything was okay. He knew me well. He'd seen the same look when Eve left me. I blew him off, telling him I had a bad weekend but everything was cool and by tomorrow, I should be back to my normal self.

When five o'clock rolled around, I grabbed my gear and left the site without saying goodbye to anyone. I just wanted to be alone. Before getting in my truck, I pulled my phone out of my back pocket and checked it for the hundredth time—there were no missed calls from Sabela. Frustrated, I threw the phone onto the passenger seat.

Normally, I would stop at a drive-thru and grab myself dinner, but I had no appetite and headed straight home instead. As I pulled into my parking space, my phone rang. I glanced over at the screen and gasped when I saw Sabela's name flash across the screen. "Holy shit!" I killed the motor and quickly grabbed the phone.

"Sabela!"

The sound of a woman crying into the phone filled my ears. "Sabela. Is that you?"

Between the tears, I heard her voice and my heart skipped a beat. "Yes."

"Oh my god, Sabela. Where are you? Are you okay?"

Her crying intensified to a frantic state. "No, I'm not okay." Her voice trembled. "I'm outside the San Diego County Jail. Can you come get me? I've been here for three days. I was arrested on my way to meeting you."

I was stunned. It never occurred to me she'd be in jail. "You've been in jail?"

I could hear the panic in her voice. "I did nothing wrong, Slater. You must believe me. My ex-boyfriend did this to me. He's fucking crazy!"

I tried to calm her down. "It's okay, Sabela, I believe you. I'm just glad you're okay. I've been so worried about you. I honestly thought I wasn't going to see you again. I can't tell you how depressed I've been."

"I'm so sorry. I had no way to call you."

After her ordeal, the last thing she needed to do was apologize to me. "Sabela, it's okay. Hang tight, okay? I'm on my way. I should be there within the hour and you can tell me what the hell is going on with this ex of yours."

Her tears began to subside. "Okay." She paused. "And Slater?"

"Yes?"

"Thank you."

"No need to thank me. I'll see you soon."

After ending the call, I got back on the road and after breaking a few speed limits, I arrived at the jail in a record time of forty-five minutes. I spotted Sabela right away, sitting on the curb, dressed in a white mini dress. She saw me at the same time and jumped to her feet. I pulled up in front of her and left the truck running as I hopped out.

I raced around the truck, where she met me halfway, and ran into my arms, kissing me hard. I kissed her back just as fervent, not wanting to let her go. "I was afraid I would never see you again," I said while gazing at her through my own misty eyes.

While holding her in my arms, I could feel the shoulder of my shirt begin to dampen from her tears. I kissed the top of her head while stroking her mangled hair, breathing in the scent. She was safe now and I would take care of her. I spoke softly as she continued to sob. "Shh, it's okay."

She pulled me closer, burying her face into my chest, her arms tight around my waist. "Slater, I'm so sorry. Please forgive me. I'm so scared. My ex-boyfriend had me arrested for stealing his car."

I tried to calm her but she wanted to tell me more.

She looked up and met my eyes "You have to believe me. I didn't steal it. He gave it to me before he left."

I gave her a reassuring hug. "I believe you."

I saw the sudden fear appear in her eyes when she told me the rest. "That's not the worst of it. He wants me to move to Texas to be with him." She took a deep breath, hesitating before she continued. "So that he would drop all the charges, I said I would." She saw how shocked I was by her sudden announcement and quickly told me more. "Slater, I don't want to go to Texas. I want to be here with you."

"Oh, thank god. For a minute there, I thought this was goodbye."

She gave me a subtle smile through her tears. "Never." And then, between her escalating sobs, she said, "He's never acted this way before. Why would he do this?"

I was trying to making sense of what Sabela was telling me, but her gushes of tears were making it hard to understand exactly what was going on. I needed to know more about this guy. "Okay. Okay, calm down," I said, seeing she was getting herself worked up again. "Let's get you in the truck and you can start from the beginning."

For the next thirty minutes, while curled up together on the bench of my truck, I listened to Sabela tell me about her ex, Davin. She started by telling me he had first called when she saw me on the beach for the first time—that explained the phone call that interrupted our first encounter. Sabela said he sounded strange, almost possessed, and was convinced she'd be moving to Texas. She went on to tell me he had called again later that night and asked if she was packed yet. When she had told him no, he became angry and demanded she'd come to Texas or she'd be sorry. Next thing she knew, she was being arrested for stealing his car.

By the time Sabela had finished telling me everything, I was furious. There was no doubt in my mind this guy was crazy. After what he had done, I had no idea what else he was capable of. He was obviously obsessed with Sabela and would go to any lengths to scare her into going to Texas. He probably thought once he dropped all the charges, she'd be so afraid that she'd do anything he asked. But there was one little thing in his plan he hadn't counted on. Me! I was now in the equation, and for him to get to Sabela, he was going to have to go through me and there's no way I was ever going to allow that to happen.

I brushed her hair away from her face and looked deep into her eyes. "I'm going to take care of you. Okay?"

She looked down and nodded. I could tell she was still feeling unsure.

I picked up her chin with the crook of my finger. Our eyes met. "I won't let anything else happen to you. You're safe now," I reassured her before leaning in and giving her a long drawn-out kiss.

"S later, I'm so scared. He has wrecked my whole life. After I called you, I called my work. They fired me for not showing up. His sister is probably gloating right now. I don't even want to go home. What if he shows up? But I have nowhere else to go. I'm not going to worry my mom with this. I can't go there, and I can't afford to move. What am I going to do?"

I had a solution and I wasn't going to take no for an answer. "I know we've just met, but I feel like I've known you forever. You said he's given you a week to move to Texas?"

Sabela nodded.

"Well, he won't be showing up before then." I hesitated, wondering how she would react to my idea. "Why don't I come stay with you at your place?"

Her eyes turned wide. "You want to move in with me?"

"I'm not leaving you alone, Sabela. If he happens to show up, which I doubt, I'll be there waiting for him. What do you say?" I asked, giving her hand an extra squeeze. I could tell she was mulling over the idea as I continued to sell her on it. "I don't have much and could be packed in an hour." I looked for any signs of agreement from her, but saw she wasn't totally sold yet. "I can tell the guy I rent my room from tomorrow. I rent by the week, it shouldn't be a problem," I added, and then anxiously waited for her answer.

CHAPTER 17

SABELA

Not only was I stunned when Slater told me he wanted to move in with me, I was also relieved. I loved his idea. I felt the same way about him—I didn't feel like I had just met him. After listening to him, I lifted my head from his chest, pulled his mouth to mine, and kissed him passionately as tears trickled down my cheeks. "I would love it," I said as I hooked my hands around his neck and pressed my forehead firmly against his. "It's bad enough I have to go back, but with you there, I'd feel much better. Thank you!"

Slater took my hands, and held them close to his mouth before kissing them lightly. "You don't have to thank me, silly," he said and kissed my hand again. "I want to do this. I wouldn't have it any other way," he added before shifting in his seat and firing up the truck. "I can get my stuff tomorrow." He wrapped me in his free arm as he pulled away from the curb. "Let's get you home and I'll order us some Chinese food. I'm sure you're starving."

I smiled, feeling grateful this beautiful man was in my life, and nestled my head in the crook of his arm. "Sounds good," I said as I closed my eyes.

It took us about an hour to get back to the duplex. Slater held me close while he drove. When we reached the duplex, he wanted to enter first and ordered me to wait outside while he made sure Davin hadn't made a surprise visit. As he unlocked the door, he said, "The first thing we're going to do is have these locks changed." He wriggled the key in the lock and spoke over his shoulder. "I have a buddy at work who's a locksmith. I'll have him come over tomorrow, if that's okay?"

With my arms folded, I nodded. "Sure." I stood frozen as I watched Slater push open the door and enter the duplex.

Nervously, I waited outside, keeping my hands locked together in front of me. Fearing Davin may be close, I found myself periodically peering over my shoulder, scanning the nearby grounds. A few minutes later, Slater reappeared and my racing heart rate began to slow.

"All clear," he said, reaching for my hand.

Relieved, I took his hand and followed him inside. For my own reassurance, I gave the room a quick scan while Slater closed the door behind us.

"I feel grungy after being in that jail all weekend. I want to take a shower. Will you join me?" I asked Slater while taking his hand. "I don't want to be away from you."

He took me in his arms and combed my hair away from my face with his fingers. "Of course. Come on, let's get you cleaned up."

Feeling lost and still a little shook up, I curled my fingers into his welcoming hand and let him lead the way into the bathroom. While still holding onto me, he opened the glass door of the shower, reached in, and turned on the water.

I was beginning to feel calmer and stood back as I watched Slater begin to undress. While standing in a trance, our eyes locked as he peeled his t-shirt away from his body and tossed it onto the floor. Instantly, I wanted to run my fingers down his magnificent tanned chest and feel his prominent abs beneath my nails. But I held back and instead, took a deep breath as I felt the ripples of excitement travel through me. I never wanted a man so much.

While I stood before him, anticipating his touch, a warm, tender smile blanketed his face as he precariously balanced on each foot to remove his jeans and then his form-fitting underwear. I smiled back followed by a tiny laugh. I took in another deep breath while I admired him, standing before me naked. Time stood still for a moment. He was perfect in every way.

With his eyes still fixed on mine, he slowly approached me, closing the gap between us. My deep breaths turned into short little pants as I felt the warmth of his breath soothe my face and the scent of his body overpower me. With my heart rate now elevated and an increased desire to be touched, Slater kissed me tenderly on my lips. It was just a light feathery kiss that brushed across my mouth, but it was enough to awaken every nerve in my body.

As we shared the same breath, our noses touching and our lips gently exploring each other's, I felt the tips of his fingers reach beneath the straps of my dress. With my eyes closed, I nuzzled my face even closer to his, nibbling on his lips with my teeth as he slowly slid the straps off my shoulders and allowed my dress to fall to the ground around my feet.

Standing before him in only my bra and panties, my nipples now hard and well-defined through the material, I melted as Slater took a deep breath and whispered in my ear, "You are so beautiful."

The admiration that shone through his eyes couldn't be denied as his stare traced my entire body. Unlike any other man I had known, he made me feel beautiful and sexy. Every inch of my being yearned to be touched by him.

With an aching anticipation, I followed his hands that were now delicately skimming the surface of the bra covering my breasts. Pausing at each nipple, he lightly circled each tip with his palms. My body became tense from his teasing light touch. I closed my eyes and held my breath as I felt the dampness between my legs began to increase.

Wanting to feel the palms of his hands against my protruding nipples, I thrust out my chest and buried my breasts in his hands. With a hunger, he pulls my bra away from my breast. My skin sizzled beneath his touch, bringing me back to our first time on the beach. But this was different. It was just us, alone together, becoming one.

His touch remained gentle, massaging my skin like I was a china doll, as he delicately explored every curve while enticing my nipples with his tongue. Stunned by the sensations rippling through my body, I froze and released a sharp gasp. Seduced by his touch, I felt weightless. My limbs melted to a relaxed state and my head was in a tailspin, high above the clouds. Unable to control my desires, I pulled Slater in close, burying his head between my breasts and clinging to his hair with my clenched fists.

He held me tight around my waist and I pushed my body up against his. Slater took one of my breasts in his mouth and began kneading it with his lips. I threw back my head and moaned with pleasure as I felt the heat from his breath blanket my skin. As he inched his way to my other breast with his tongue, I let out another moan while still clasping on to his hair with my curled fingers.

In an attempt to control my elevated panting, I pressed the floor with my feet as I dug my nails into Slater's back. Slater sensed my hunger for him and tugged harder on my breast, causing me to release a loud hiss of satisfaction. I didn't know how much longer I could hold out. I whispered in a heated breath, "I want you."

Slater rose his head and devoured my lips, exploring the back of my mouth with his tongue. Using his body weight, he pushed me against the counter, his now prominent erection probing between my legs. I grinded my hips, riding him between my panties, coating the tip with the damp satin material. Slater groaned as his hands gripped my breasts, squeezing them sensually as he kneaded them with his palms.

Melting beneath him, I began rotating my hips faster, pressing my magical spot against his groin. Slater let out a long moan of pleasure. "Oh yeah," he said, and with short quick jerks, began thrusting his hips between my thighs.

Again, I gasped, but this time much louder. "Slater! I want you."

Slater broke free from our kiss, leaving me breathless and my heart racing. In a rushed state, he pulled me away from the counter and with one swift movement of his fingers, unsnapped my bra and ripped it away from my body. A second later, he grasped the edges of my panties and quickly rolled them down my legs to my feet. In haste, I stepped out of them.

Slater breathed heavily as I stood before him, naked, itching to be taken by him. Reading my mind, he pulled me in close, our bodies moist with sweat, as he traced the outside of my lips with his tongue. "Come on. Let's take a shower. I want to have my way with you."

I tossed my head back and laughed. "I can't wait."

Pleased by my confession, he echoed my laugh and released the hold he had on me, but only long enough to take my hand and lead me into the now steamy shower.

Once the glass door was closed, I pressed my back against the chilled tile and allowed the beads of water to cascade over my skin. Slater watched, his eyes filled with desire as I stood there, teasing him. I wondered how long was he going to resist me?

Closing my eyes, I turned and held my face up under the flowing water, shaking my wet hair down my back while pushing my breasts close together and squeezing them tenderly. It didn't take Slater long to approach me and grab me from behind. I spun around to meet him and lost myself in an alluring kiss as the water cascaded over our faces. I was lost in his embrace. Nothing else mattered. He had totally seduced me and I was all his for the taking.

While kissing me, he reached over my shoulder and grabbed the liquid soap. I stood, motionless, as he flipped open the lid and poured some of the gel across my chest. Slowly, it began to ooze between my breasts. Slater stopped it and smeared it over my skin, working it into a soapy lather. "Hmmm, that feels good," I moaned with my eyes closed.

"Shhh," Slater whispered as he continued to caress me with the soap.

I stood before him, highly sensitized by his touch as he drowned me in the lather, gliding his hands over my entire body before rinsing me down. "Turn around," I heard him whisper in my ear.

I obeyed with no questions, and faced the wall.

I felt him close behind me, our skin almost touching. I shifted on my feet, anticipating where he was going to touch me, and then I gasped. "Oh, Slater!"

"Shhh, Sabela," he whispered again as I felt the tip of his finger trace the crack of

my butt cheeks down to my hungry sensual core. His touch was soft but ignited every nerve in my body, sending a wave of juices to my center. I spread my legs a little further, letting him know I was ready to take him. But he was taking his time. It was his turn to tease me. I let out a sequence of muffled moans as his finger entered me and began to explore. I pushed down hard on his hand, wanting to feel his finger deep inside of me. I was not disappointed. With force, he buried it in as far as he could, and I released a loud moan of satisfaction. He quickened his pace, thrusting deep inside. I pushed down harder and circled my hips in rhythm to his movements. "Slater, I want you inside of me!" I cried.

Driven by the passion in my voice, Slater fulfilled my desires and with ease, inserted his magnificent shaft into my now drenched core. A deep, guttural moan escaped from his mouth as he felt the warmth between my legs engulf him. I bellowed a loud scream of satisfaction as my limbs melted into a jellylike state, and panted repeatedly as Slater quenched my hunger for his manhood.

"Oh my god, Slater! Don't stop," I begged.

Consumed by my appetite for him, Slater increased the speed and force of his thrusts, bringing me over the edge within minutes. Unable to control myself anymore, I reached around and grasped his hands as my body flinched and exploded into a rocketing orgasm, led by high-pitched squeals of pure bliss.

Enticed by my wave of orgasmic happiness, Slater continued with his fiery thrusts at an even faster pace. I knew he was close to coming, I could feel it. His breathing was becoming heavier. His grunts were louder. I held my breath and froze, anticipating the moment, and then with one last powerful push, he released himself inside of me, followed by a boisterous moan.

He stayed buried in me for a few minutes, his arms hanging limp around me. "Wow!" he said in a satisfactory tone. "That was amazing."

"It was," I agreed as I slowly eased myself free. I turned to face him and smiled.

He threw me a loving grin and embraced me in his arms before kissing me on the lips. "Come on. Let's go to bed. I want to be holding you as I drift off to sleep."

CHAPTER 18

SLATER

J couldn't believe what this Davin guy had done to
Sabela. What a fucking jerk! I turned and glance at the
digital clock next to the bed. It was two thirty in the goddamn
morning, and I was still wide awake, thinking about what I'd like
to do to the asshole. I peeked down at Sabela. I couldn't see her
face in the darkened room as she lay curled in my arms, but the
softness of her breathing told me she was sound asleep.

I gently kissed the top of her head while softly stroking her
hair. "I'll protect you, Sabela," I whispered. "The asshole better not
show up here, if he knows what's good for him," I added under my
breath before finally slipping into a deep sleep while still holding
my girl.

The next morning, I woke to an empty bed. Sabela was gone. I
glanced over at the

clock. It was seven. I panicked, pulled off the covers, and
jumped to my feet. Racing through the duplex, I called out her
name. "Sabela!"

I let out a huge breath of relief when I found her in the kitchen,
looking as gorgeous as ever. Her hair was uncombed and she wore

only an oversized white t-shirt while fixing coffee. I rushed to her side, took her in my arms and held her tight. "Oh god, Sabela. You scared the shit out of me." I said in a panted breath while stroking her hair. "I freaked out when I woke up and you were gone."

"I'm sorry. I couldn't sleep," she replied before meeting me in a pleasant morning kiss. "I keep thinking Davin is going to show up here any day now. He's expecting me to go to Texas."

Her eyes couldn't hide the fear she was feeling.

"What are we going to do if that happens?" She didn't wait for me to answer, her voice raising a notch. "He had me thrown in jail for something I didn't do, Slater. I'm scared of what he might do next."

I held her close in my arms; my body was her shield. I wasn't going to let anything happen to her and spoke with an edge to my voice. "If he shows up here, Sabela, I'll be here to protect you." I sensed she was doubting my promise as I struggled to find the right words to comfort her. "Nothing is going to happen to you. I won't let it."

She pulled away from my hold and looked at me. I could see the fear was still in her eyes. She didn't believe me. "Slater, you have to go to work today. I'll be here alone." She grabbed her hair and pulled it back away from her face before leaning against the counter and folding her arms. "What if he comes while you're gone? I don't want to be here alone." Her fear turned to anger. "Oh, and I have no car now." She shook her head in disbelief. "I can't even go anywhere if I wanted to."

I approached her and pulled her in again. While stroking her shoulders, I gave her a confident smile. "Trust me, I've thought about that and I've already told you, I'm not going to let you out of my sight." I paused, contemplating telling her my plan. "You need a job, right?"

Sabela threw me a puzzled frown. "Yes."

"Well, do you want to work with me on the job site?"

Sabela slapped my chest with the palms of her hands and

laughed out loud. "Are you crazy? I'm not a contractor. I can't build houses. Slater, what are you talking about?"

I grabbed her hands in midair and pulled them to my chest. My stare caught her attention. "Sabela, you know how to paint, right? Walls and stuff."

She thought for a moment. I could tell she was wondering where this was going. "Well, yeah."

I smiled, knowing my idea may work. "I bet I could get you a job as a painter."

Sabela laughed while trying to break free of my hands. "Now, hear me out," I said holding her hands tighter. She stopped struggling and listened. "Drew, the foreman, is a pretty good friend of mine."

Sabela finally looked intrigued "Okay. Go on, I'm listening."

"I'm going to call him and explain to him what's going on. I'll try and persuade him to hire you." I paused to make sure she was following. "That way, you'll never be out of my sight and you'll have a job," I told her, feeling pleased with myself. I knew it was a good solution. In fact, it was the only one we had. I just had to convince Sabela. I stood there, naked in the kitchen, feeling a bit chilled while I waited patiently for her answer.

She paced around the kitchen, contemplating my idea.

"Come on, Sabela. I'm getting cold here. What do you think?"

She chuckled at my remark. "Hold on, I'm thinking." Then, added jokingly, "And besides, I like seeing you naked in my kitchen." She paused again. "I don't know, Slater. Wouldn't I be the only woman there? I'd feel really uncomfortable."

I spun her around to face me, trying desperately to get her to agree. "Yes, you would be. But, you'd be with me and you'd be safe. You won't be alone. I can't think of a better plan." I wasn't going to take no for answer. and took the initiative. Feeling confident, I broke free from our embrace. "I'm going to get dressed and give Drew a call right now. I want to bring you to work today. Otherwise, I'm taking the day off. I told you, I'm not going to let you out of my sight."

Sabela raised her hands in defeat. "Okay. I'd be really surprised if he hires a woman, though. In the meantime, I'll make you some coffee." She let out a giggle. "Wait! I don't even know how you like your coffee."

"Black," I replied before scurrying out of the kitchen, in a rush to call Drew.

After throwing on my jeans and a t-shirt, I grabbed my phone off the end table and made myself comfortable on the edge of the bed before dialing Drew's number. Three rings later, he picked up. "Drew here."

"Hey, Drew, it's Slater."

"Hey, Slater. What's up, dude? Hope you're not calling in sick. We've got a deadline to meet today."

"No. No, Drew. I have a favor to ask you."

"A favor?" He hesitated. "What do you need."

I paused for a minute, running the question through my head. "Well, my girlfriend is having some problems with her ex."

Drew interrupted me. "Girlfriend? I didn't know you had a girlfriend."

"Yeah, I do," I quickly replied, trying not to lose my train of thought. "Anyway, he's been threatening her. In fact, she lost her job because of him and, to be honest, I'm afraid to leave her alone. I wondered if you could give her a job as a painter at the site?"

Drew let out a loud crackle of a laugh. "A painter. Has she ever painted anything before?"

"No, but anyone can paint. Come on, Drew. What do you say? I've never asked you for anything before. Help me out here, bro."

I heard a long, heavy sigh through the phone as he considered my request, and I held my breath as I waited. "I don't know, man. You're asking me for a huge favor. I've never hired a woman before. She'll be the only girl on the site and I don't want her to be a distraction. I also don't like the idea of some crazy ex hanging around. I don't want any problems on the job, Slater."

"There won't be any problems. I promise, and I can guarantee he won't be coming around. He's all the way in Texas. It's a long story. I can fill you in with all the details when I get there. Just do this one thing for me. Please," I begged.

Again, I heard his heavy sigh. "All right, Slater. I'll help you out."

Relieved and excited, I yelled into the phone, "Yes! Thank you, Drew."

But Drew quickly silenced me with his adjusted stern tone. "But...any problems, Slater, and she needs to go. Do you understand?"

I brought my own tone down a few notches. "Yeah, sure, I understand. I'll make sure of it, I promise. And thanks, Drew. I owe you one."

"No problem. Looking forward to meeting this girlfriend of yours. I'll see you guys soon."

After ending the call, I did a little happy dance before rushing to the other room to tell Sabela, where I found her sitting on the couch, drinking coffee while watching the morning news.

She stared at me with a creased brow. "Well?"

I thought about teasing her for a while, but I couldn't hide my excitement. "You got the job! You are now officially a painter."

The dropped jaw, along with the raised eyebrows, told me the news had shocked her. "What! You're kidding me?"

"Nope. I'm not kidding. Come here and give me a kiss," I said, extending my arm.

In one quick dash, she was in my arms, beaming. Feeling triumphant, I picked her up and spun her around in my arms as we kissed.

"Wow! I never thought he would go for it." She laughed. Once back on the ground, she gave me another kiss, this one softer than the previous, and smiled. "Thank you, Slater."

I smiled back, relieved she wouldn't be out of my sight. "You're welcome." I took her hand and began leading her to the bedroom. "Now, come on. We have to find you some painting clothes. Jeans and a t-shirt will do. And you need to tie your hair back. Don't want to get any paint in that beautiful hair of yours."

"I like the casual dress attire." Sabela laughed while searching in the closet for the appropriate wardrobe.

Thirty minutes later, we were ready to go. Before heading out the door, I had to pause for a minute and take Sabela in my arms one more time. "You are the cutest goddamn painter I've ever seen," I said before kissing her tenderly on the lips. "Drew said he didn't want you to be a distraction." I let out a callous laugh. "Do you know how hard that's going to be?"

She laughed. The smell of her sweet breath captured my attention.

"The question is, can I paint?" she asked jokingly.

I took her hand and began leading her to the front door. "There's nothing to it. I'm sure you'll be a master at the trade."

"We shall see," she replied as we headed to my truck.

CHAPTER 19

SABELA

I was shocked when Slater told me I had the job. As much as I appreciated him persuading his boss to hire me, I was nervous as hell. Me! A painter! I've never painted a goddamn thing in my life, except for my bedroom walls with my dad when I was kid. I hope they're not expecting the next Picasso from these hands. Being the only woman on the site will be somewhat intimidating, but I'll just have to cling to Slater like a lost puppy.

I didn't want to dampen Slater's overjoyed mood with my concerns and decided to keep them to myself. On our drive to the job site, he wore a permanent smile, and sang to tunes blasting from the radio, which quickly uplifted my spirits. I didn't want to crush those feelings. The important thing was, I had a job again and could pay my bills, and now that Slater was living with me, things would be a lot easier.

Twenty minutes later, we were pulling into the site. Slater turned to me and took my hand. "Are you ready to start your new job as a painter?" he asked, followed by a tender kiss on my cheek.

I gave him a nervous smile. "Sure. Let's do this."

When we stepped out of the truck, I suddenly became unsure

of this crazy idea. Surrounded by noisy, heavy equipment, cement trucks pouring concrete off to my left, and the strange looks I was receiving from some of the crew as they walked by, had me feeling alienated.

Slater picked up on my uneasiness and took my hand. "You'll be okay," he said with a reassuring smile while holding out his hand. "Come on, let's go to Drew's trailer and introduce you."

I welcomed the support and grasped his hand tight. "Sure."

A few minutes later, we were standing in Drew's trailer, also known as his office. We found Drew slumped at his desk, peering over his glasses, looking at confusing construction plans. He was younger than I had imagined. Probably in his mid-forties. His dark brown hair was cut short, away from his face. He looked to be in good shape and pictures of his wife and kids were prominently displayed on his desk, showing the world what a proud family man he was.

Still holding my hand, Slater introduced me. "Hey, Drew. This is Sabela."

Drew looked up while removing his glasses and stood to greet us. "Well, hi, Sabela. It's nice to finally meet you. Slater has been keeping you a secret."

I laughed at his comment as I walked over and nervously shook his hand. "Hi, Drew. Good to meet you too."

Slater followed suit and approached Drew's desk. "I really appreciate this, man. There won't be any problems, I promise."

Drew nodded. "We won't get into any details right now," he said before returning to his seat. "You can fill me in later. I'm happy to help out." He then turned to me and gave me a big friendly smile. "So, Sabela, are you ready to show me your painting skills?"

I gave him a nervous laugh. "I'll do my best."

Satisfied with my answer, he rubbed his hands together, eager to get us started. "Okay then. Unit number six is ready to be painted," he told Slater. "Some of the guys are already over there. I'm going to have you guys join them." Verifying we understood, he gave us both a glance.

Slater nodded. "Sure."

Drew returned his focus to Slater as I listened in. "You can help with the spray painting and we'll have Sabela do the detailed stuff, using a roller and paintbrush."

Slater snuck me a wink when Drew said my name, and I threw him a discreet smile.

When Drew was finished, Slater gave him another nod before taking my hand. "You got it, boss," he said before leading me out of the trailer.

Once outside, Slater gave me a smooch. "Are you doing okay?"

"I'm great." I loved how he was always looking out for me.

"Okay. Just checking," he said, giving my hand an extra squeeze.

On our way to the condo, more of the crew passed by. Some looked puzzled by my presence, while others couldn't resist boosting my ego by giving me a wolf whistle. Slater and I laughed at both reactions.

When we reached unit six, Slater led the way through the open double front doors, where we found ourselves standing in the main room. I noticed all the windows were covered with plastic.

Five guys stood there, in white paint suits, which covered their regular clothes. A few were speaking in Spanish and joking around, but that soon ended when I entered the room. Silence invaded the air except for the sound of classic rock playing from the radio in the kitchen. The work crew didn't move. They looked at me with their eyes wide, like I was some sort of ghost. I giggled at their reaction as Slater slid his arm around my waist and pulled me in closer to his side.

"Hey guys. This is Sabela and before you get any ideas, she's mine," he said, as he looked at me with pride in his eyes.

I smiled back, showing him the same pride.

He turned away and spoke to the men. "Anyway, she's going to be working with us from now on."

Slater's announcement instantly started some chatter amongst the guys, but he wasn't finished speaking and rose his voice a notch so he could be heard. "I don't want any of you giving her a hard time. It's her first day and I'm sure she'll do a great job. And we're going to give her all the support we can." He glanced across the room, making eye contact with each worker, and then added, "Right, guys?'

With no arguments, the guys all nodded in sequence. The tallest and heaviest, spoke first. "Sure, man, not a problem. I'm Enrique."

I nodded back and gave him a friendly smile. "Hi, Enrique."

Another of the men spoke. He was skinny and much younger. Probably in his early twenties. He brushed back the bangs of his hazelnut-colored hair. "Hi, I'm Ricky."

I nodded and smiled again. "Hi, Ricky."

The three remaining guys, all with dark hair and probably in their mid to late twenties, welcomed me and told me their names, which were Danny, Marco, and Eddie.

After the formal and somewhat uncomfortable introduction, Slater waved the head painter—Enrique—over and shared with him his plan. "I'm going to let you guys spray the downstairs while Sabela and I work on the upstairs."

Enrique nodded and then continued listening.

"I need to finish tiling in the master bath and I can have Sabela help me. "Then we can come down here and paint the window frames and doorjambs while you guys go upstairs and spray the four bedrooms." Slater thought it was a good plan. "How would that be?"

"Sounds good," Enrique replied with another nod.

"Great," Slater replied, while grabbing two white suits out of a box by the front door, and a couple of masks. He then turned to me and smiled. "Come on. You get to be my assistant today."

I followed him up the stairs that led to a large landing and then through the double doors on the left, into the master suite. Once inside, he closed the two doors behind him, threw down the painting suits, and pulled me into his arms. He let out a loud laugh before planting a juicy wet kiss on my lips.

"Did you see the look on their faces?" He let out another laugh while throwing back his head. "They were drooling like puppies." Slater then traced my lips with his finger. "I bet they've never seen such beauty before," he said before kissing me again.

I pulled away and slapped him playfully on his chest. "Oh, stop. I'm probably the first woman they've ever seen on the job."

"Well, that too. But I can tell they all wanted you." He chuckled.

"You know, I thought I wasn't supposed to be a distraction. And here you are, kissing and hugging me," I told him with a hint of sarcasm.

"I said it wasn't going to be easy." He sighed between words, then glanced toward the master bath. "But you're right. Let's get to work. I'm going to have you help me finish up the tiling."

I placed my hands on my hips. "I know nothing about tiling. You know that, right?" I said to him—this time, using a serious tone.

He snickered at my concern. "Don't worry about it. I'll do all the hard stuff."

I liked his answer. "Well, that's good to know," I said, and gave him a satisfactory nod. "So, what do I get to do?"

"I'll have you hand me the tiles and wash off the excess grout when ready, and you can also change out the buckets of water when needed."

"That all sounds easy enough."

Slater turned around and grabbed the suits he had thrown onto the floor. "Come on, let's get you suited up."

Being an amateur, it took me a while to get the white suit on over my clothes. But when I had, I couldn't resist, checking myself out in front of the large mirror spanning the wall behind the double sinks. I laughed at my reflection as I held my arms out like a bird. "Well, this is a fashion statement and a half."

Slater approached me from behind, hugging me around the waist and nuzzling his face into my neck. He looked at me in the reflection. "I think you are the cutest goddamn worker here."

I stared back at him. "Hmm, you're not so bad yourself."

Slater let go of my waist and spun me around. "Okay, you're distracting me again. The guys will be up here before we manage to get anything done." Trying to break the spell I had on him, he pulled away and quickly clapped his hands. "Let's get to work," Slater said while slipping into his paint suit, and pulling up the zipper. "There's no need to wear the masks yet. We only need them when they begin spraying up here."

For the next couple of hours, I saw, for the first time, what a patient man Slater was. Not knowing anything about his trade, he took his time explaining to me everything he was doing. He didn't make me feel stupid and even praised me numerous times when I picked up easily on a task. I must say—this was a nice change from working at the dentist, where I spent most days looking in people's mouths and smelling their stinky breaths. *I could get used to this.*

Once the tile job was completed, we cleaned up the mess and left the room. The rest of the house smelled like paint fumes and Slater told me to put on my mask, which I did, but I soon discovered talking through the mask was difficult, and began laughing.

"Why are you laughing?" Slater mumbled from behind his mask.

"It's hard to talk with one of these things on."

He shook his head. "Oh, you'll get used to it. Come on, let's go downstairs and join the guys for lunch. Afterwards, we'll be painting downstairs, while they go upstairs."

"Okay," I agreed.

Relieved to take the mask off, even after a short time, we joined the rest of the crew outside on the back patio to eat our lunch. I wasn't one to keep much food in the house—I had a bad habit of always eating out—but like every household, I had a jar of peanut

butter and a jar of jelly, and quickly whipped up a couple of sand-
wiches for our lunch before we had left.

We found the men scattered on the low walls of the patio that
separated it from the grassy area of the backyard. Sticking close to
Slater, we found our spots and sat down. I discovered I had no
reason to be nervous. The guys were super friendly and made me
feel welcome. Slater held the entire conversation, explaining what
Davin had done and why I was now working at the site. All the
guys shook their heads in disbelief and offered to help in any way
they could. In other words, they would help kick Davin's ass.

Enrique was the locksmith Slater had mentioned, and he
agreed to come back to our place after work to change the locks.
Feeling relieved, I thanked him profusely, knowing I would be able
to sleep that night. I honestly didn't think Davin would show up at
the duplex, but then again, I never thought he would have me
arrested and thrown in jail. I had a distinct feeling I hadn't heard
the last from him.

After lunch, the guys lugged their gear upstairs, leaving Slater
and I alone to do the detailed painting downstairs. Before putting
on my mask, Slater took me in his arms and kissed me gently on
the lips. "Are you still doing okay?" he asked.

Again, he was looking out for me. "Yes, I am," I told him before
kissing him back. "The guys are awesome. Thank you for getting
me this job."

"Will you quit thanking me?" He brushed a strand of hair away
from my face. "I'm doing this because I care about you and I'm not
going to let anything happen to you."

While wrapped in his arms, I couldn't help but feel safe. I
trusted him and gave him a long, lingering kiss. Lost in the
moment, feeling the touch of his lips against mine, my skin began
to tingle as I felt myself being aroused. I pulled him in closer and
wrapped my arms around his neck while searching for his tongue.
Through his white suit, I could feel his prominent bulge pressing
up against my thigh as he kissed me with more force while

pushing me back against the wall. Locked in a passionate kiss, I locked my legs around his waist, pressing harder against his rising bulge with every thrust.

Pinned against the wall, Slater took both my hands and held them high above my head, locking me into place as he covered my neck with his warm breath and wet kisses. I moaned with pleasure as my body yearned to be touch by him.

"God, I want you," Slater whispered in my ear.

In a panted breath, I whispered back, "I want you too."

Overpowered by his hold, I strained my neck and closed my eyes as I braced my body against the wall. Slater took advantage of the only exposed skin on my body and began sliding his moist tongue across my neck, licking every exposed inch, followed by small nips of his teeth and soft kisses. Again, I moaned with pleasure as the heat within my body began to rise.

As he continued to tease my neck and face, awakening every nerve I owned, I peeked out of the corner of one eye and looked up the stairs, surprised to see Ricky frozen midway up, looking down at us. We were being watched and instantly, I was turned on even more. He didn't know I saw him. I whispered in Slater's ear, "Don't look and don't stop, but we're being watched by Ricky."

Slater paused for just a moment as he listened carefully to my words. When a devious smile appeared on his face, I knew he understood. He whispered back, "Well, let's give him something to look at. We both know how much we love to be watched." He laughed quietly.

I giggled as Slater pushed me harder against the wall and began to moan louder in between the deep kisses he was now giving me. Keeping my arms pinned above my head with just one hand, he used the other to caress my body in a frenzied state. Through the material of the paint suit, he cupped my breast, massaging deeply while squeezing my nipple with his fingers. I moaned with pleasure as my back arched against the wall. Unable to use my arms to embrace him, I lifted one of my legs up high and hooked it around his thigh, pulling him in closer. Slater thrust his groin into my body, grinding his hips across my pelvis. I breathed heavily as he searched for my tongue.

Feeling his hand glide across my body, using deep, circular motions, sent waves of heat to my most sensitive areas. I was aroused to the core and unable to stop. I opened my eye slightly and peeked in Ricky's direction. He was still watching us with a dropped jaw and wide eyes. Fearing he might get busted by another worker, Ricky quickly checked the top of the stairs to make sure no one was coming. Satisfied, he resumed his focus on us while adjusting his manhood beneath his painting suit.

Slater continued to caress me in all the right places while keeping me pinned to the wall. Using feathery strokes, he used his tongue to stimulate the soft spots behind my ear and then slowly followed my neck line to work on the other ear. I turned my head in frustration, straining my neck as I felt his warm breath hit my skin. I wanted to reach out and squeeze his body hard, to feel his flesh in my hands. I was desperate to reach down and grasp his growing bulge and massage it tenderly in my palms. I wanted to moan louder than I was allowing myself to, but knew I had to restrain myself, and the restrictions just made me want him more.

My breathing was intense now. I could feel a tingling beginning to stir between my legs. I held my breath as it began to travel up past my stomach and across my chest and over my nipples. I knew what was coming next and said to Slater, my tone desperate, "Kiss me! Kiss me now!"

Slater didn't hesitate. He knew I was about to orgasm and covered my lips with his as my body tensed up before it shuddered from the waves of orgasmic bliss. Using his lips as a blanket to shield my voice, I released controlled shrieks and gasps, trying my best not to be heard. But Ricky heard me. I knew he did because as soon as my orgasm was over, I heard the scurry of his footsteps racing up the stairs.

Slater finally released my arms, and like a rag doll, I fell into his embrace, giggling. "Fuck! I can't believe I just came," I said, in between panting breaths. "I Wonder what Ricky is thinking right now?" I laughed. "You know he'll never be able to look us in the eyes again."

Slater stroked my hair, and kissed the top of my head while I rested it on his chest.

"I know, poor kid," he said sarcastically. "We've probably traumatized him for life. It's all your fault," he joked.

I raised my head from his chest and gave him a playful evil stare while placing my hands on my hips. "*My* fault?" I threw him a cocky laugh. "Ha! *You're* the one that pinned me against the wall, mister."

He gave me a peck on the lips. "Well, if you weren't so goddamn irresistible, I might be able to control myself. And then you tell me Ricky is watching us. Well, that was it for me. I was instantly turned on." He threw me a cheeky smile. "And I know you were too."

"Yeah, I liked that he was watching. It reminded me of our time on the beach," I said, feeling my cheeks warm.

Slater glanced at his watch. "Come on, Miss Distraction. We'd better get to work." He tickled my waist. "I could fuck you all day, but duty calls."

I jerk my body from his tickling hand. "Okay, boss."

For the next few hours, Slater and I painted window sills, doorjambs, and anything else that couldn't be done with a sprayer. It was an easy job, not requiring much skill and in no time, Slater had enough confidence in me to finish the task on my own, while he worked on the tile job in the entrance way.

It was no surprise to me that we didn't see Ricky for the rest of the afternoon. The poor kid was probably too embarrassed to face us after watching me have an orgasm. *I wonder what's going through his mind at this very moment?* For me, that was part of the turn-on— the shock factor it brought to those watching us, and knowing those images would stick with them for a long time was pure satisfaction.

When five o'clock rolled around, the crew began to make their way downstairs. I had already taken off my suit and mask, and was waiting for Slater, who was busy talking to Drew on the phone. Enrique approached me, his hair speckled with paint, and he told me he would be at our house in an hour to change the locks. I thanked him and told him I would tell Slater.

The last one to come down was Ricky. I couldn't help noticing how hard he was trying to avoid eye contact with me. Amused by his shyness and embarrassment, I decided to make it even harder. I looked him in the eyes while giving him a devious smile. "Goodnight, Ricky."

He stopped two feet in front of me, unsure where to look, and lifted his head just enough to acknowledge my presence. He spoke so quietly, I barely heard him. "Good night, Sabela."

I knew it was wrong of me to keep teasing him but he was making it too easy, so I continued to toy with him. Using a sweet flirty voice, I spoke to him again. "I'll see you tomorrow."

"Yeah, see you tomorrow," he muttered, keeping his eyes fixed to the floor as he retrieved his ice chest and headed out the front door.

A few minutes later, Slater hung up the phone and approached me. His smile never failed to warm my heart. He took me in his arms and kissed me tenderly. "So are you ready to go home?" he asked.

"Yeah. Enrique said he would meet us in an hour to change the locks." Then I laughed.

"Why are you laughing?"

"Oh, poor Ricky. He's so embarrassed. The kid couldn't even look at me when he came downstairs. I shouldn't laugh but you should have seen his face. When he saw me, he didn't know where to look. It was quite comical."

Slater joined me in my laughter. "Oh, he probably couldn't wait to get home and jack off. He has plenty of material to last him for a lifetime. He'll never have a problem coming again."

I slapped his chest, shocked by his comment, and shrieked, "Slater!"

"What? You know I'm right. Come on, let's get home. We don't want to miss Enrique."

CHAPTER 20

SLATER

*O*ver the past two weeks, Sabela and I lived like a regular married couple. Still unsure of Davin's next move, we've done everything together, from working, shopping, laundry at the local laundromat, and if we managed to be up before the sun, we'd take a morning jog on the beach before work. Surprisingly, Davin hadn't made any more threats since Sabela was released from jail, but I wasn't ready to let down my guard just yet. Having the locks changed eased our minds considerably, but we still hadn't gotten around to changing her cell phone number. We needed to do it soon.

Living at the duplex hasn't been easy for us. For me, it would always be the place Sabela shared with Davin. It will never feel like our home. But I was there for her. Knowing how uncomfortable she now felt, I asked her if she had any friends she could stay with, but she wouldn't have it and insisted on staying with me. If I could, I would get us a new place tomorrow, but I just don't have that kind of cash laying around. For now, we're stuck here.

Sabela showed me a photo of this guy, Davin. He didn't look like anything I had imagined and my first thought was, *What the hell did Sabela see in him.* He certainly wasn't a tough guy, dressed in a dorky white shirt and ugly yellow shorts. I was certain he'd never flexed a muscle, with those skinny arms of his, and his pasty white legs didn't look any better. I would have no problem taking this guy on, that's for sure. But someone would have to pull me off him before I beat him to a pulp for all the shit he's done to Sabela.

I studied the picture some more. His eyes definitely looked shady—I could tell he wasn't all there in the head. I mean, come on. No normal, sane guy would have his ex-girlfriend arrested for a crime that never happened. But a sick motherfucker would. What bothered me the most though was, I had a feeling we hadn't heard the last from the asshole. I wondered what he would try next? Whatever it was, he was going to have to get through me first.

Being with Sabela just felt right. She was perfect in every way and I couldn't imagine my life without her. I would protect her, no matter what. In such a short time, our relationship had grown so much. I knew it sounded crazy, but I already knew I wanted to spend the rest of my life with her. She just didn't know it yet. I was doing my best to take things slow but it wasn't always that easy.

A few weeks ago, after a passionate night of lovemaking, I held her in my arms, and as I smelled the sweet scent of her hair, I told her I loved her and waited for her reaction, not knowing what to expect. Fears were roaming inside of me that I may have come on too strong, too soon, and had probably scared her off. But I was wrong. She reacted in the way I had hoped. Feeling her body relax against mine and her breasts pressed closer against my bare chest, she raised her head and told me she loved me too. Hearing those words was sheer bliss. I felt my life was finally complete.

She was doing so well on the job site, and I could tell she loved it and was having a good time. She was learning new things every day and her enthusiasm showed she was eager to learn more. Not only could she paint well using a paintbrush and roller, but she now knew how to use a paint sprayer too. She was also getting to be real handy with tools; in fact, she'd become an expert on the chop saw, and had no problem using the staple gun. Even Drew was impressed with her newfound skills.

Everyone on the job has treated her with respect and made her feel welcome. No one has given her a hard time. I must say, I'm proud of my co-workers. Ricky is still having a rough time feeling relaxed around her though, and stutters when he speaks to her. I can't help but laugh a little when I see his nervousness.

For the sake of Ricky's sanity and probably the other guys too, Sabela and I now restrain ourselves from having heated moments on the job. Even though I want to jump her bones every time I look at her, we'd be screwed if we lost our jobs—no pun intended. Drew was a forgiving guy, but having sex on the job might be asking a little too much from him. Even though we managed to behave at work, we still had some wild moments on the beach in our secluded spot, while others watched.

I couldn't explain why we loved to be watched by strangers. We only knew what a big fucking turn-on it was and it was totally freeing. It was also a hell of a lot of fun and harmless.

Tonight, we were celebrating the end of a busy work week with a couple of Sabela's friends. She'd invited them over, along with their significant others, for dinner and a game of Monopoly. Sabela loved board games—as for me, I hadn't played one in years. I was looking forward to a night of dinner and games with some new friends. I'd never met the couples, but Sabela used to work with the girls at the dentist office and has kept in touch with them since she got fired. If I remembered correctly, their names were Jill and Cathy. Sabela reminded me that she'd never told either one of them about her time in jail or that Davin was behind it. Mainly because Davin's sister, Claire, still worked at the dental office with them, and as far as Sabela was concerned, the less she knew, the better.

It was to be our first dinner party together since I'd moved in. After work, we stopped at the store and picked up the fixings to make a spaghetti dinner, along with a couple of bottles of red wine. Sabela insisted on making the dinner, so I left her in the kitchen while I went and took a shower. Within a few minutes, I heard tunes playing from the CD player and Sabela singing joyfully to the songs. It warmed my heart to hear her so happy. Knowing she was content, I stepped into the now steaming shower.

Ten minutes later, feeling fresh and squeaky clean, I wrapped an oversized bath towel around my waist. I combed my wet, matted hair vigorously in front of the mirror before beginning the dreaded tedious task of shaving, something I'd always hated doing and many times I won't shave for almost a week. As I stood there, the aroma of spaghetti cooking in the kitchen began to drift into the bathroom, and I breathed in deeply to capture the scent. A smile spanned across my face as I heard Sabela's sweet voice singing to the music. *At this moment, life was pretty good.* While contemplating the joys of life, I suddenly heard Sabela scream from the kitchen, followed by a petrified "No!" and a loud crash.

In a state of panic, fearing what I might find, I threw down my comb and raced to the kitchen, where I found her shaking and crying uncontrollably while hiding her face in her hands. I raced to her side and took her trembling body into my arms, trying to console her. "Sabela! What happened? Are you okay?" I asked in a fretted state.

She didn't seem cut or injured in any way, but something caused her to scream. As soon as she was wrapped in my arms, she squeezed me tight and buried her head in my chest, not wanting to let go.

Confused and worried, I scanned the kitchen for any broken dishes or spilled food but saw nothing. Still holding her in my arms, I stroked her long mass of hair that was hiding her face. I searched the floor frantically and finally spotted her cell phone face down on the other side of the kitchen, like it had been thrown. I wanted to go pick it up, but Sabela needed to be held right now. I had a feeling my answer to her distressed outburst was on that phone.

I gave her a little shake. "Sabela, tell me what happened. You're scaring me."

Her body continued to tremble as she kept her head close to my chest. I tried to raise her head but she resisted. In between her tears and gasps for air, she spoke with undeniable fear. "It's Davin." She sniffed hard. "He texted me."

Her words froze me. "What?"

"I'm scared, Slater. He's coming to get me."

I released my hold on her and grabbed the phone off the floor. I turned it over and read the text on the now cracked screen. It was written in capitals.

DON'T MAKE ME COME OUT THERE, SABELA. WE HAD A DEAL!!!

I stared at the screen in disbelief. "What the fuck!"

Sabela was petrified. She held her clenched fists to her chest and forced herself to speak. "He's coming here." She looked at the phone in my hand. "That's what it says."

I slammed the phone face down on the counter and took her back in my arms. She curled into my body, seeking comfort from my embrace. Her sobs tore at my heart. *Davin would pay for this!*

"Shhh. It's okay," I whispered. "I'm not going to let anything happen to you. The guy is crazy." I massaged her back with deep, penetrating strokes as I tried to console her. "We've had the locks changed. He can't get in here and tomorrow, we're going to get your number changed." My voice rose a notch, angered we hadn't done it yet. "Something we should have done a long time ago."

I raised her head, forcing her to meet my eyes. "Look at me," I said with urgency.

She lifted her eyes and met mine. I felt the fear she was feeling by the way her body trembled, and by her sunken, sad eyes that were now drenched with tears. I shook her shoulders gently with both hands, gripping her flesh. I wanted her to believe me. "I'm not going to let you out of my sight." I gave her another little shake. "You are safe with me."

Tears continued to roll down her cheeks. Softly, I wiped one a way. "You have to believe me."

She nodded. "I do." She buried her head in my chest again. "I'm scared, Slater," she choked. "What if he comes out here?"

I nestled my face in her hair as I pressed my lips firmly on her head. "Then I'll be here waiting for him."

She wasn't convinced. "I don't want to stay here anymore." Then she told me what I already knew. "We have to find a way to move."

I had to be honest with her. "We will, soon." I rubbed her shoulders to reassure her. "But we don't have the cash right now, sweetie."

"I know. But I can dream, can't I?"

I had an ideal. "What about your mother?"

Sabela raised her head. "What about my mother?"

"I know you had said you wouldn't stay with her because you didn't want to worry her…"

Sabela cut me off. "Yes, I did, and I still won't stay with her, Slater. I'm not dragging my mom into this shit."

She told me her mind was made up and I wasn't about to try and change it. Instead, I took her hand and kissed her gently on the lips. "Don't let him scare you." I kissed her again. "For all we know, he was just fucking with you by making some stupid empty threat."

Sabela shook her head. "I'm not sure about that. He accused me"—she pointed to her chest firmly with her finger— "of stealing his car, and I then lied to him, so he'd drop all the charges." She folded her arms across her chest and spoke with a snarl. "I can guarantee, he's pissed at me. Clearly, Davin is not to be made a fool of. I'm seeing that now."

I was determined not to let this guy come between us, or threaten Sabela with a measly text, and stood my ground. "Don't let him get to you, Sabela," I said, unfolding her arms and closing in on her space. I kissed the tip of her nose. "That's what he wants."

She giggled and I finally saw a smile break through.

"Don't let him ruin our night," I said, smiling back.

She suddenly remembered we had company coming tonight and pulled her head back. "Oh god, I don't feel like entertaining now." She glanced at the clock on the wall. "But it's too late to call anyone. They'll be here in half an hour."

I changed my tone to an assertive, happier one. "Now, come on. Pull yourself together and go take a quick shower. It will make you feel better." I glanced over at the stove. "It looks like you have dinner under control"—I looked at the table—"and you have the table set."

She forced another smile.

"While you're taking a shower, I'll get dressed and finish up," I told her before taking her back in my arms. "What do you say. Are we going to have a good time tonight?"

She nodded. "Yes, we are." She smiled again. This time, it was a little bigger. "I love you."

"I love you too," I replied, before giving her a playful smack on her behind as she turned and walked away.

CHAPTER 21

SABELA

*A*fter leaving Slater in the kitchen, I broke down once more in the bedroom while undressing. I was petrified of what Davin may do next. I wasn't sure how long I stood in the middle of the room, naked, clutching my waist and holding myself tight while I sobbed. But soon, the chill of the surrounding air forced me to pull myself together and run the shower. Once the water had reached the perfect temperature, I stepped in, closing the door behind me. The warm water cascading over my body instantly calmed me, and I closed my eyes as it trickled over my face. My mind was racing with so many *what if* thoughts about Davin and what he might be capable of.

I wondered how this would have played out if Slater hadn't come into my life. Alone, with no job, and having to deal with continuous threats from Davin. Would I have gone to Texas? A small part of me believed I would have. I wouldn't have known what else to do. Now I know that will never happen. I love Slater and knew we weren't going to let Davin come between us. But I couldn't help thinking, how was this all going to end? I wouldn't move to Texas, but it was obvious Davin wasn't taking no for an answer. That was what scared me.

My lips curled into a smile when I thought of Slater. I closed my eyes briefly in gratitude. I couldn't believe he was still with me through all this shit. He had such a big heart and right now, he was my rock and I'd be lost without him. Most guys would probably have left running by now, not wanting to deal with drama from an ex. But poor Slater uprooted his own life to come live here with me and protect me from the devious threats of Davin. *God, I love him so much.*

After a quick shower, I wrapped myself in a towel and looked in the mirror—I didn't like what I saw. My eyes were red and swollen. Anyone would know I've been crying. I braced the sink with my hands and leaned in closer to the mirror, speaking to my reflection. "Come on, Sabela, pull yourself together." Determined to hide my fears, I grabbed my hairbrush and pulled it through my wet, matted hair with force.

After applying an extra layer of makeup around my eyes to hide the redness, I tugged on a pair of blue jeans, a comfortable, loose, gray sweater, and after one final check in the mirror, I felt ready to greet Jill and Cathy.

I found Slater at the table, adding last-minute touches to the setting. From across the room, I admired him, enjoying the warm, tingling sensations his presence was causing.

Hearing me, he looked up and gave me a warm smile that melted my heart. "Hey, beautiful. Are you okay?"

I approached him, instantly feeling safe when he wrapped me in his arms and kissed me

softly on the top of my head. I nuzzled into his chest, feeling overpowered by his masculine scent. "Yeah, I'm okay." I glanced over his shoulder. "The table looks great."

"You do too," he said before breaking free. "Now, come on. Let's get you a glass of wine and more relaxed before your friends arrive." He grabbed the bottle of wine and began pouring me a glass. "Oh, by the way," he said, grabbing my attention, "I turned off your cell phone and threw it in a drawer, and it's going to stay there until we exchange it tomorrow."

I didn't argue. I thought it was a great idea. But I was afraid my mom might try and call, and may become worried when she couldn't get a hold of me. "I have to call my mom as soon as I get my new phone," I told Slater.

He was busy topping off the glasses and tilted his head my way. "Sure," he said as he set the bottle down and handed me a glass. "When was the last time you saw her?"

Anxiously, I took a large gulp before answering, savoring the juices as they traveled down my throat, giving me the lift I needed. "Gosh, come to think of it, the last time was when I took Davin"— I cringed when I said his name— "so she could say goodbye to him." I let out a sarcastic laugh. "Ha! She loved Davin. God, if she only knew what a monster he turned out to be. She, too, was fooled by him and has no idea what's going on." I took another sip of wine.

"So, you've not seen your mom since we've met. Right?"

"I've spoken to her on the phone a few times, but I've said nothing about my time in jail or what Davin is doing to me." I raised my voice a few notches. "Slater, I can't tell her. She'd only worry." I looked at him with pleading eyes while placing a firm grip on his arm. "We must keep this from her. But if I don't see her soon, she'll begin to suspect something is wrong." I threw Slater a subtle smile. "I think it's time you met my mom."

Slater rolled his eyes and laughed. "I would love to meet your mother. But first, I'm about to meet your friends," he said, setting down his glass.

Between Slater's gentle ways and a good glass of wine now inside of me, I was soon beginning to feel the stresses of the day subside.

A few minutes later, the doorbell rang. Slater stood behind me as I approached the door and reached for the handle. I took a deep breath for courage and felt the gentle squeeze of Slater's hand on my shoulder. "You'll be okay," he said softly.

I turned to face him. "Only because you're here." I took another deep breath and opened the door, squealing. With my arms stretched out, I used the most pretense voice I could muster up. "Cathy!"

Cathy hadn't changed. Her hair was still dyed bright red, and she was still wearing the gaudy oversized necklaces. She greeted me with matching open arms and embraced me, giving me a tight, friendly bear hug. "Sabela! I've missed you," she cried, matching my tone.

My sinuses were smacked with her heavy perfume, bringing me back to my days at the dental office. We always knew when Cathy had entered the building. I turned for a minute and held my breath. "I've missed you too!" I said, trying desperately not to breathe in the overwhelming scent.

Behind her stood her husband, Gary, who hadn't said a word. After releasing my hug from Cathy, I skimmed by her and gave him a peck on the cheek. "Good to see you, Gary."

Being the quiet one in the relationship, he simply nodded and quickly pushed his glasses back onto the bridge on his nose after they had slipped from his nod.

I motioned them in with my hands and introduced them to Slater. I had filled Cathy in over the phone on my new relationship, asking her not to tell Davin's sister, so she wasn't surprised by his presence.

Slater offered them both a glass of wine and instantly engaged everyone in small talk. Smitten by his charm, I left them and went and checked on dinner and refilled my glass. While waiting for our other guests to arrive, we all moved to the table and began engaging in witty conversations. A few minutes later, we were interrupted by the chimes of the doorbell. I excused myself and greeted Jill and her boyfriend, Travis, in the same manner I had greeted Cathy.

Jill was wearing her trade mark pink colors and bling, bling jewelry. I've never known anyone who loved pink as much as Jill. Even her car was pink. Her and Travis had been dating for a while and I wouldn't be surprised if they ended up tying the knot. After confirming how much we all missed each other, I led them both to the table, introduced them to Slater, and set them each up with a glass of wine.

Travis was a stocky guy with some muscle. Like Slater, he dressed casual in a black t-shirt and jeans and his light, wavy brown hair rested on his shoulders. He also worked in construction and immediately bonded with Slater. I didn't know Travis that well. Our friendship always consisted of a casual hello whenever he was with Jill, but when he discovered I was now working with Slater, he saw me in a new light, almost with admiration, and spent most of the evening complimenting me and offering me all kinds of tips and advice. Jill and Cathy, on the other hand, couldn't hide the disbelief from their faces when they learned I was now a painter, and that I was also cutting wood and using a chop saw, along with many other new skills Slater was teaching me. I also sensed they may have been a tad jealous.

Hanging out with friends was just what I needed to escape the nightmares of Davin. We laughed, we joked. We talked about the good old days of working together at the dentist office and because Slater didn't know me back then, he was amused by some of the stories we told.

After a hearty spaghetti dinner, more wine, and full bellies, we played a two-hour game of Monopoly that resulted in Gary winning. I discovered Gary also had a passion for board games, and playing them bought him out of his shell. No longer was he the quiet Gary I had always known. In fact, he was the loudest player at the table, cheering and yelling words of triumph each time one of us landed on his property. He played the greedy landlord quite well.

By the end of the night, I was sorry to see everyone leave. The duplex soon fell quiet and my mind shifted back to the threats of Davin. Slater already knew me well and saw the change in my mood.

"Come here," he said, holding out his arms.

I gave him a subtle smile and caved into his embrace. His strong, muscular arms wrapped around my body felt like a shield of armor, and I wished I could stay there forever. "I love you, Slater."

"I love you too. It's going to be okay. I promise," he told me while tightening his hold.

I wrapped my arms around his waist and pressed my cheek close to his chest. The sound of his heart beating in my ear soothed me. "I'm so glad you're here with me. I don't know what I'd do without you."

Using the tips of his fingers, he gently raised my chin until my eyes were looking at his, and he kissed me softly on the lips. "Come on, let's go to bed. I want to lay with you and hold you tight until you fall asleep in my arms."

CHAPTER 22

SLATER

*T*he next morning, I woke with Sabela still wrapped in my arms, her face of innocence still resting on my chest. Even while I had been sleeping, I refused to let her go. I stared down at her beautiful face, looking so peaceful as she slept. The fear she was feeling had shown through last night, but looking at her now, it had disappeared. I wanted her to be free of the terror that was constantly overpowering her.

I gently brushed a strand of her silky hair away from her eye, and she stirred from my touch. "Hey, sleepyhead," I whispered as I leaned in and kissed her cheek.

She opened her eyes and smiled. "Hey," she whispered back.

Aroused by her beauty, I lifted her chin with two fingers until she was

facing me, and kissed her passionately on the lips. She welcomed my affection and with her

free arm, wrapped her hand around my neck, and pulled me in closer, searching for my tongue with hers.

Tangled in the bedsheets, I pulled them free from our bodies. While still kissing her, I rolled her onto her back and laid on top of her, pressing my naked body against hers. The touch of her velvety skin ignited the burning desire I had to be inside of her even more. Every time I was close to her, I wanted her. I was obsessed.

In a circular, rhythmic motion, I thrust my groin between her legs. With her eyes closed, Sabela moaned with pleasure while massaging my body with hers. I moved away from her lips and traced the contours of her neck with my tongue, down to her now erect nipples, circling each one with a swift fluttery motion before smothering them with my mouth. I felt her body relax beneath me as she welcomed my touches of seduction. Wanting to taste more of her, I gripped the flesh on the sides of her waist and slid my body down over hers until my lips were touching her stomach. She let out another moan of pleasure.

I inhaled her scent as I teased the soft skin around her belly button with delicate kisses. Her body swayed back and forth, her hips circling beneath me in response to my touch. I reached down and found her inner thighs. With ease, I slid my hand between them and gently separated her lips while briefly brushing the tips of my fingers against her now moist center. The circular motion of her hips increased as I stimulated her with my hand, using my fingers to enter to her. Welcoming me, she spread her legs wider and pushed her back into the bed.

While still caressing her abdomen with my tongue and lips, I inserted my fingers deeper inside of her. She raised her head and gasped, "I want you."

My erection was now at its peak. I could feel the beads of sweat forming on my forehead as I began grinding my hips across her body. After a few more thrusts of my fingers, I slowly guided the tip of my throbbing erection to her and let it slide in.

Long moans of pleasure escaped us as I savored the warmth of her inner walls engulfing me. I didn't want this moment to end. She felt so good. Wanting to be deep inside of her, I began thrusting my hips while tantalizing her erect nipples with my tongue. Her moans became stronger and louder as I thrust harder and quicker. Wanting to feel all of me, she arched her back and spread her legs wider. I thrust deeper into her while taking the mounds of her breasts into my mouth, burying my face in her flesh. She let out another gasp and raised her hips higher. I couldn't hold out much longer and began riding her harder and faster, thrusting myself deep inside of her with each push until I came.

I felt her body tense up beneath me and freeze for just a moment. I knew she was about to come and remained inside of her, stimulating her breasts with my tongue and stroking the inside of her with my still throbbing shaft. Within a few seconds, she took in a deep breath and exhaled a loud scream as her orgasm overpowered her, sending her body into movements of quick, sharp jolts, each one followed by a loud gasp of ecstasy. As her orgasm began to subside, she moaned with pleasure, looking completely satisfied and wearing a huge smile of content.

Feeling limp, my body completely drained, yet not wanting to pull away, I remained inside of her for a few more minutes as I looked down at her beautiful face. "Now, that's a good way to start the day." I chuckled before kissing her tenderly on the lips.

Melting my heart, she gazed into my eyes and wrapped her arms around my neck before kissing me back. "I agree. I could get used to this." She laughed.

We stayed in each other's arms for a while longer, both feeling completely satisfied after our session of lovemaking. Being with Sabela just felt so right. We were so in tune with each other. I'd never felt this way about anyone, not even Eve. I felt like I'd known her much longer than the short time since we had met. I knew she was the one and I wasn't about to let Davin destroy us. I would do anything to protect her and keep her in my life.

The first thing on my list was to get her a new cell phone. I figured we could do it on our lunch break. God, how I wished we had the money to move to a new place. The thought of him knowing where she lived had me concerned, and Sabela had also told me there are too many memories here of Davin that she'd sooner forget. I had to find a way to save some money and get her out of here, but we were barely getting by as it was.

I kept my thoughts to myself and reluctantly pulled myself away from Sabela. "Come on, pretty one. We've got to get ready for work." I stood up from the bed and stretched. "I'm going to take a shower," I grinned. "Want to join me?" I asked, feeling my sexual urges beginning to stir again, just from the thought of caressing her with soap.

With a bounce in her step, she leaped out of the bed and skipped over to me, pressing her fine, naked body against mine and wrapping me in her arms. "You bet! I've not had enough of you yet." She laughed while giving my butt a hard squeeze.

Like a drooling puppy, I followed her into the shower where another round of sensual lovemaking took place. Thirty minutes later, we found ourselves running late for work, and dashed around the duplex in a frenzy, gathering our coffee, lunch, and the tools needed for the day, both of us laughing at our distractions that morning.

When lunchtime rolled around, I was excited about getting Sabela a new phone and felt somewhat at ease when it finally happened. Pleased she not only had a new number but a brand new phone too, I forwarded the threatening messages from Davin to my phone, before handing in the old one.

Before returning to work, Sabela made a quick call to her mom and told her a small white lie—that she had lost her phone, and gave her the new number. Her mother didn't question her story and Sabela promised to visit her soon, telling her she had a surprise for her. I chuckled when Sabela threw me a sexy wink at the mention of a surprise.

On our way, back to work, I looked over at Sabela. "It's great we changed your number and all, but it still bothers me that Davin knows where you live."

It was obvious from the way her body jolted up straight and the look of fear that invaded her face that she hadn't given it much thought. "Oh my god, Slater! He could be watching us, every time we leave the duplex."

She squeezed my arm tight and I winced from the pain of her nail digging into my flesh, but said nothing. I didn't know why I brought it up and now wished I never had, but I was concerned.

Her eyes were now big and round. "I don't want to go back home."

I released her grip and took her hand. "Hey now. It's going to be okay. I've told you, I'm not going to let anything happen to you." I gave her a little smirk. "And besides, I doubt he would fly all the way from Texas just to stalk you."

Sabela shook her head in disagreement and raised her voice. "I didn't think he would have me thrown in jail either, but he did! I thought I knew him. But I don't. He's a monster and I have no idea what he's capable of, Slater." Unable to control her tears, she clung to me, not wanting to let go. "We have to move. I won't feel comfortable until we do. What are going to do? I'm scared."

I didn't have the answers, but wished I did. I'd never been one to save money, always living paycheck to paycheck. Now, I wish I had. The only thing I could do right now was console her. "Shh, it'll be okay. I'll think of something. I promise," I told her, pressing my face against the top of her head and holding her tight, wondering how I could come up with the money to move.

CHAPTER 23

SABELA

I thought everything was going to be okay once I got a new phone. Davin could no longer harass me, and Slater and I could go about our lives and look forward to building a future together. But I was still living in the place I had shared with Davin. More than anything, I wanted to move but I didn't want to go anywhere without Slater. Sure, I could probably move into my mom's, but like I said, I didn't want to worry her. Slater and I were in this together and we would get through this.

But now, I'm more paranoid than ever. As we drove back to work, I found myself looking inside all the other vehicles around us, expecting to see Davin in one of them, peering straight at me with revenge bleeding from his eyes. I shuddered at the thought and cowered in my seat.

Slater tried to comfort me and make me feel better as best as he could, but he couldn't get inside my head and make the terrifying thoughts go away. I clung to him for the entire trip back to work, not knowing how I was going to go back to that duplex tonight. It no longer felt like home and I was trapped with no way out. God, I just wanted all of this to go away. I wished Davin would just leave me alone. Even hundreds of miles away, he was making my life a nightmare when I should be enjoying my newfound love with Slater. I thought I knew Davin. How wrong I was and to think I had seriously considered moving to Texas with him, months before he left. Thank god I came to my senses.

The thought of talking to Davin's sister about his threats had crossed my mind briefly. But, she never really talked to me and I think it was because I was dating her brother—so why would she believe anything I had to say—so I soon trashed that idea.

For the first time, I didn't want five o'clock to roll around. I kept wishing time would stand still and I could remain at work forever, where I felt safe. I was quiet for the rest of the day, keeping to myself while painting the trim in unit number seven. Slater picked up on my somber mood and tried his best to cheer me up, but with no success. I gave him a weak smile periodically but it wasn't genuine and he knew it.

After work, he insisted on taking me out to dinner and I didn't object. I knew he was procrastinating going home because of my fears and I appreciated his efforts, but we couldn't eat out every night. I had to pull myself together and get over the paranoia I was feeling, but not tonight. I'll start tomorrow. Tonight, I wanted to enjoy a nice peaceful dinner with my sweetheart and not listen to my head.

After a scrumptious seafood meal at a restaurant overlooking the ocean, we took a romantic walk on the beach to watch the glorious sunset. It was breathtaking to see, and being alone with Slater was just what I needed. Holding hands, we walked barefoot where the ocean met the sand, mesmerized by the changing colors of the sky. It was the perfect ending to an upsetting day, until I realized we had nowhere else to go but home.

As Slater drove us back to the duplex, I curled up close to him, feeling protected wrapped in his arms. When we pulled into our parking space, I felt my anxieties beginning to return. My palms became sweaty and my heart began to pound at an accelerated rate. Slater noticed the change in my body language. I was tense, and I hesitated before opening the truck door.

He reached over and placed his hand on my shoulder. "Hey, it'll be okay. He's not going to come here."

My back was toward him. I didn't turn around. I simply rolled my eyes and stared straight ahead. "How do you know that, Slater? You don't know that for sure."

He knew I was right and didn't have an answer. Silently, he opened his door and stepped out of the truck.

"You go first," I said as we approached the front door.

Slater shook his head and for the first time, showed his frustrations with my constant fears. "I think you're overreacting just a bit. He would have come here by now. Trust me."

I couldn't blame him and didn't try to defend myself. The fact that he was still with me, sticking by my side through all this shit, told me he cared. The minute the front door of the duplex sprung open, I gave him a gentle shove. "Go on. I'll wait here."

As I waited outside the door with my ears pinned and chilled from the cool air, I had second thoughts about allowing Slater to enter the duplex alone. I should have shown him some support and gone in with him. After all he'd done for me, I was disgusted with my cowardness. I had left him to conquer his—my— battles alone. What if Davin was in there? Hiding and waiting for us. Suddenly I had a terrifying thought. He could have jumped Slater and knocked him out cold, and I would never know it.

I yelled through the doorway. "Slater! Is everything okay?" He didn't respond, and I yelled again, this time, a little louder. "*Slater!*"

From the other end of the duplex I heard his voice and held my chest with relief. "It's all clear! You can come in."

I entered with caution and did my own scouting around the front room, checking every visible space before being convinced Davin wasn't here and I felt comfortable removing my jacket.

Things were quiet over the next week. One night, Slater and I were doing laundry at the local laundromat and I had this eerie feeling I was being watched, but we were the only ones inside. Slater was sitting on the bench, his back to the window that looked out to the parking lot, and I was standing while folding clothes. I glanced out the windows—the sun was setting and the skies were turning dark quickly. The lights had come on in the parking lot, and that's when I noticed a male standing beneath one, looking directly into the laundromat. He was wearing a large overcoat, which I though was odd because it wasn't that cold out, and he had the collar pulled up high around his neck, like he didn't want to be recognized. I stared for a few minutes, and when I saw the way he stood, with his legs crossed at the ankles, I knew it was him and screamed. "Oh my god! It's Davin!"

Slater jumped to his feet, the magazine he was reading fell to the floor, and he rushed over to me, pulling me into his arms. "What? Where?" he asked in a frantic state while peering out the window, looking in the direction where my wide eyes were glued, my fears having been confirmed.

I huddled close to Slater, burying my head in his chest and when I looked up, Davin was gone. I pointed with my finger. "He was right there. Looking right at me. I know it was him." I tugged on Slater's sweater, insisting he believe me. "He stood with his feet crossed at the ankles. Only Davin stands likes that."

Slater freed himself from me. "Wait right here," he ordered, and scurried out the double glass doors. I watched, glued to my spot as he scanned the parking lot in both directions, and then quickly came back in. "There's no one out there except a couple of teenagers smoking cigarettes. Are you sure you saw someone?"

"Yes, I'm sure. It was him. I told you he'd be back." Then I started to doubt myself. Maybe I *was* just being paranoid. But I know what I saw and because of it knew I didn't want to go back to the duplex that night. "Slater, I don't want to go home. He may be waiting for us." I had an idea. "Let's go to my mother's. He'll never show up there."

"Your mother's? I thought you didn't want to worry her."

"I don't and I won't. I'll put on a front and use the excuse that I wanted her to meet you, and that we just needed a weekend getaway."

As always, Slater didn't argue and was the most understanding guy I had ever known. After rushing to finish up the laundry and get out of there, Slater and I had our clean clothes loaded in the truck within ten minutes. Tailing close behind Slater, we both scanned the parking lot with our final loads but saw nothing. Slater quickly fired up the truck while I called my mom, who was thrilled to learn she was going to have company for the weekend. I played the part, sounding cheerful, telling her I had a new boyfriend I wanted her to meet, but the truth was, I was a friggin' mess inside. My stomach was churning like I was about to throw up, and I couldn't stop my hands from shaking. Thankfully, my mom didn't seem to notice the nervous quiver in my voice.

I didn't calm down until we got on the freeway. I held Slater's hand tight as we drove through town, scanning every vehicle, looking to see who was inside. I glared at every person on the sidewalks, but I didn't see the man I saw in the parking lot and began to question myself. Was it Davin I saw? If it wasn't, then why was he dressed so oddly for a warm night, and why was he looking directly at me? And then there were the crossed feet. I was convinced it had to be him. There was no other explanation.

By the time we reached my mom's, I had managed to calm myself down completely with the aid of Slater's reassurance and with his continual comforting embraces, letting me know he wasn't going to let anything happen to me.

That evening, he was the perfect boyfriend, catering to my mom's every need. How could Mom not love him? She even surprised me the next morning, while Slater was still sleeping and we were alone at the dining room table, having coffee. "I like Slater much better than that Davin guy you were dating. I never did like him."

"You never told me that, Mom. I thought you always told me everything."

"Well, I didn't want to hurt your feelings. You were obviously smitten by the guy." Mom took a sip of her coffee and savored it for a moment. "But there was something about him. It was those eyes of his, I felt like he was looking straight through me." She shuddered. "Gave me the creeps."

I couldn't believe how well she had read Davin. She knew him better than I did. I hadn't seen what she had so clearly. Maybe I just didn't want to. I nodded, followed by a subtle smile at her observations, and listened as she continued to share her thoughts on my choices of men.

"Now, Slater, on the other hand. He's a keeper." She smiled through her words. "He's genuine. He's not hiding nothing from you. I can tell he loves you. I can see it in his eyes when he looks at you. Your eyes are the gateway to your soul, my dear. When he looks at you, it reminds me of your father and how he used to look at me." She let out a heavy sigh. "Oh, how I miss your father."

I reached across the table and took her hand. "I miss him too, Mom."

The wounds of losing Dad last year were still raw for the two of us, and would probably never go away anytime soon, if ever. It was still hard to talk about, and I found myself choking up every time. He was building a storage shed in the backyard when he had a heart attack and died at the young age of fifty-one, leaving Mom a widow at forty-nine, and me without a father at twenty-three.

When my mom called me that morning, hysterical and in tears, I left work immediately and raced over to the hospital, but he was already gone by the time I arrived. I was devastated I had never gotten to say goodbye. Mom was trying to pick up her life and live without Dad in it, but the sadness in her eyes never left. After taking two months off from work, she returned to her job of fifteen years as a bank clerk. I was there for her as much as I could be and for now, will never move too far away.

Something Davin should have understood. And as much as I love Slater, I wouldn't move more than hour away from mom if he asked me to. Which got me to thinking—what were we going to do once our current job wrapped up? Even though that wouldn't happen for at least another six months, it was something to think about.

I didn't tell Mom I had been fired from the dental office because she would have wanted to know all the details. Instead, I told her I had quit. I saw the disappointment in her eyes and it stung a little. She knew how hard I had worked to get my degree as a dental assistant and didn't understand why I had given it all up to work in construction.

Making excuses, I simply told her it was difficult to work with Davin's sister and to tide me over, Slater was nice enough to get me a job at the site until I found work at another office. To my relief, she bought it. Would I ever return to the dental field? Honestly, I didn't know. As surprised as I am, I love working in construction. There's so much to learn and every day, I'm learning something new. The best part was, I got to spend my entire day with Slater.

It was hard to leave my mom's knowing we had to return to the duplex. The weekend went by far too quickly, but I managed to pull myself together and rise above the fear I was feeling, with the help of Slater and knowing I would be safe as long as he was with me.

Today, he's going to teach me how to lay a laminate floor in unit number six. This was going to be the model unit for future showings and was near completion. But construction would continue at the site for the next six months while future tenants were being targeted.

When we arrived at unit six, Slater was pleased to see the flooring had already been delivered and was neatly stacked in the center of the main room downstairs, and another load had been placed in the master bedroom upstairs. We decided to tackle one of the smaller bedrooms upstairs first and began by stacking some of the boards outside the door before taking measurements of the floor space.

Within an hour, and because of Slater's expertise in coaching, I had the system down. To my surprise, laying a hardwood floor was quite simple. It kind of reminded me of the game, *Tetris*. Feeling confident to leave me alone for a while, Slater left to go check on the guys who were spray painting another unit. A couple of new guys were hired today and he wanted to make sure they were settling in okay and handling the job. After confirming, "I got this," he took off his tool belt, laid it outside the door, and told me he'd be back in twenty minutes.

Feeling proud of myself, I simply nodded while crouched over a board, banging it into place. When I stood up, he had already left, and I proceeded to exit the room and grab another board. Within a few minutes, I was in the same position, my back toward the door, kneeling over and knocking another board into place with a rubber hammer. While engrossed in my work, even though there were no words spoken, I felt the presence of someone behind me.

Without looking, I assumed it was Slater. "Back already?" I hollered over the loud music coming from the radio. There was no reply. I stopped what I was doing and looked over my shoulder, shocked to see a man dressed in a paint suit and wearing a mask standing in the doorway. "Oh, hi. You must be one of the new guys. You're in the wrong unit. They're painting unit number nine today. If you go out the front door, it's three units down on your left."

He didn't answer. Thinking he didn't hear me over the music, I stood and walked over to the radio to turn it off. When I turned around, the man was now in the room and had closed the door behind him. Feeling uneasy, I stepped back a few paces. "Can I help you? I told you, they're painting in unit number nine."

He remained silent and kept his eyes fixed on me from behind his mask. As he took a few steps closer, I glanced over at the rubber hammer lying on the floor across the room, wishing I had it in my hand. I took a few more steps back until I was stopped by the wall behind me. "I said, you're in the wrong unit," I repeated, fear clearly detected in my voice.

Bracing the wall with the palms of my hand, I watched as the man began to remove his mask, and then I gasped in horror.

"Hi, Sabela. It's been a while," he said with an evil grin smeared across his face.

"Davin!" I screamed, quickly scanning the room for an escape, but he was standing between me and the door.

CHAPTER 24

SABELA

I watched with horror, my heart hammering beneath my chest, as he let his mask drop to the floor and slowly began walking toward me. "Surprised to see me? We had a deal, Sabela. Do you think I was just going to forget about it while you shacked up with your new boyfriend in *our* home? Yes, I know all about you and your new beau." His eyes narrowed. "You've hurt me, Sabela. I thought you loved me." His voice began to crack. "I came back a few weeks ago. I just wanted to talk to you, but then I saw you with *him*," he snarled.

I said nothing as he told me he had been stalking me.

He drew his face close to mine and hissed when he talked. "I followed you and watched from the parking lot while you canoodled with that man over a candlelit dinner. Then, I watched you do laundry together. How sweet," he said sarcastically. "I should be with you. Not him," he added, raising his voice. "I love you. Don't you understand that?"

I *knew* it was him I had seen at the laundromat. I cowered against the wall, my body tensed with fear, afraid my knees would collapse beneath me. I scrambled for words to reason with him.

"Davin, we agreed to end our relationship. We said our goodbyes at the airport. Why are you doing this? I don't want to move to Texas. My life is here. My mom is here. You know I can't leave her," I begged, desperation flooding through my voice. "Surely you understand that?"

He ignored my reasoning and his mood suddenly switched to anger. He raised his voice, the rage in his eyes penetrating me like a sharp knife. "Shut up, Sabela! A deal is a deal. I left here with a broken heart. I tried to forget about you, but every girl I meet reminds me of you, and I get angry at them and do stupid things." He shook his head at his confession.

I tried to talk to him some more. "What stupid things, Davin?" I asked, puzzled by his remark.

He ignored me. "You're coming home with me, where you belong. I've been watching you for a few days now. Laughing and giggling with your new beau when you leave in the mornings to come here. and I must say, it's pretty easy to get a job here," he said, sounding pretty proud of himself. "All's I had to do was tell the big guy. What's his name?" He paused for a minute. "Drew. That's it. I simply had to tell Drew I'd been painting since I left high school." Davin let out a cocky laugh. "What an idiot. He didn't ask me for any references or have me fill out any kind of application. He just shook my hand and told me I was hired. A piece of cake. And now"—he snarled his last few words— "I'm here to take back what's mine."

He stood within inches of my face. I had nowhere to go. I pressed my back hard against the wall. "Davin, let's talk about this. You're scaring me," I pleaded.

He reached out and curled a strand of my hair around his finger. "Oh, Sabela, I'm done talking. You had your chance but you chose to ignore me." He shook his head from side to side. "That wasn't very smart of you."

I whipped my head back, leaving a few strands of my hair wrapped around his finger, and winced from the sudden sharp pain of my hair being ripped from my head. "Don't touch me! I'm not yours!" I yelled.

With a sharp toss of his head, he laughed out loud before stroking his finger down the side of my cheek. I cringed and quickly turned from his touch. His smirk disappeared from his face and was replaced with a thin snarl after my rejection. He squinted his now darkened eyes, and spoke slowly, with an evil tone.

"Now, you know I always get what I want. I made it completely clear to you that I wanted you to move to Texas and because you didn't listen, I had to come all the way here to bring you back. I'm not happy about this, Sabela. Why are you making everything so difficult?" Suddenly, he reached down and grabbed my arm. I winced again from the pain as he pulled it up and clung onto my clenched fist. "You had to piss me off, didn't you?"

Trying to ease the pain that was shooting through my arm, I bent my body at the waist and leaned into his pull. "I'm sorry, Davin. I had no idea. I didn't mean to. But I can't go to Texas."

He tugged at my arm again, pulling my body up with force until my now moist eyes were level with his. I shied away from his stare, but he shook my arm fiercely, forcing me to look at him. With a hard shove, he used his body to push me against the wall. My back crashed against the hard surface and I groaned as I felt the sharp shooting pains travel up my spine. Still holding my clenched fist, he placed his other forearm across the front of my throat, pinning me. I tried to wriggle free from his grasp but it only caused him to push harder.

"You're mine, Sabela. When are you going to realize that? Stop fighting this. I love you, don't you understand that." He shoved me once more. "Stop trying to fight what we have."

"No, I'm not yours!" I yelled, struggling to break free from his hold by wriggling my body and kicking with my legs. I tried pulling his arm away from my throat with my free hand, but my attempts only stirred his anger even more. Drowning in fear and my body trembling uncontrollably, I was afraid of what he was capable of. Would he seriously hurt me? Using more of his strength, he prevented me from protesting with my body by pushing his forearm harder into my throat. I coughed from the pressure.

"Stop, you're choking me. I can't breathe," I begged while trying to pull his arm off, but it was no use—he just pushed harder, not acknowledging my cries.

Unable to say any more words because of the pain in my throat, I simply gave him a long, cold stare. He smirked before kissing me hard on my lips, pushing my head against the wall. I tried to break free, but it was impossible. I held my mouth closed tight, scrunching my face in protest as I felt his lips touch mine. I tried to scream through my clenched mouth, but only managed to muffle high-pitched screeches of horror as he continued to press his disgusting lips against mine. After what seemed an eternity, he finally pulled his mouth away.

"Get off me!" I yelled into his face, followed by fierce coughing.

"You're mine! Don't you forget it, Sabela!" He laughed out loud and again smothered me with his mouth.

As I tried to free myself from his grasp, with no success, I could feel my head beginning to spin from the pressure of his arm digging into my throat. I didn't know how long I could remain standing, and felt myself beginning to fade. Was I going to pass out? I couldn't let that happen. Who knows where he would take me. I had to remain conscious. I had to stop him somehow. I could feel him kissing the side of my neck but I had no strength to fight back. My eyes were beginning to feel heavy. I strained to keep them open. Was that his tongue I felt sliding down my neck, over my skin? Silently, I shuddered as I felt tears roll down my cheeks.

I was trapped and couldn't do anything to stop him. He continued to keep me pinned against the wall. My knees felt weak as he lowered his head down to my breasts. The sound of his breathing intensified until it almost sounded like a pant. His hot breath saturated my chest as I felt him following the contour of my breast through my shirt with his tongue. "I'm going to fuck you, Sabela, and take you back. I'm going to claim what is mine." I didn't answer. I couldn't answer. He shoved his forearm even deeper into my throat. "Do you hear me?" he growled.

I could only manage a whisper. "Yes, I hear you."

I tried to pull away as he buried his face into my breasts, sliding his tongue across the material over my nipples, but it was no use. He teased one of the nipples with his teeth and I froze as he nuzzled deeper into my bosom and nibbled on the nipple. I tried to scream for help, but only choked and coughed from the sharp pain buried deep in my throat.

I closed my eyes, hoping it would be over soon, but then, a large crashing sound startled me from my drowsy state and I was suddenly free of his grasp. I heard a male voice yell, "What the fuck is going on here! Get the fuck off her!"

As soon as I was free, I slid down the wall and collapsed on the floor, sobbing and holding my body tight, while coughing uncontrollably. Through my matted hair hanging in front of my face and the flood of tears, I looked across the room and saw Slater wrestling with Davin. Slater had pulled him off me by the scruff of his neck and thrown him fiercely to the ground. But even though Davin was a scrawny-looking guy, he was putting up a fight. Davin was on his back, his hands in front of his face.

"Who the fuck do you think you are? You fucking piece of shit!" Slater yelled, with fury in his eyes, before throwing a punch to Davin's face.

I cowered even closer to the floor and crawled over to the corner.

"Fuck, man!" Davin yelled back, before swinging his fist at Slater and hitting him hard in the stomach. Slater wasn't fazed by his blow and cold cut him again in the face. This time, he drew blood. I watch in horror as it poured out of his nose. But Slater wasn't done. Davin tried to shield his face with his arms and hands, but Slater stood and began kicking him hard in the stomach. "You fucking asshole. You're going to jail for this, you motherfucker!"

Suddenly, Davin was on his feet and threw a sharp punch to Slater's cheek. I screamed as I watched Slater fall to the ground. For a minute, he was stunned, holding his face as Davin began kicking him in his ribs. Slater curled his body and winced from the pain.

"Slater, get up! "I screamed. "Please, Slater, get up!"

Slater must have heard my voice. He shook his head as if to bring himself back to the moment, and grabbed Davin's ankles. With a sharp tug, he pulled him to the ground and, without missing a beat, Slater pulled himself up and began swinging fiercely at Davin, hitting him wherever he could with his fist. His face, his stomach, his head. After each blow, Davin became weaker, his own swings becoming less frequent. Blood now spilled from Davin's mouth. He strained to keep his eyes open, fluttering them shut between blows. Soon, he was no longer fighting back. He was out cold, laying limp in the middle of the room, blood splattered across his face and over his shirt.

Panting from shortness of breath, Slater slowly came to his feet. I could tell he was hurting. He moved like an old man, bent over and holding his stomach. He looked down at Davin with disgust and snarled before giving him one last kick in his abdomen.

"You piece of shit!" He then turned to me and stumbled over to where I was. He crouched before me, taking me into his arms. "My god, Sabela, are you okay?"

Once in his arms, I felt safe and just collapsed, letting the tears flow like a faucet. I couldn't stop and held on tight to Slater, digging my nails into shoulder. "I am now. Oh god, Slater. He was like a monster. It was like he was possessed." I buried my face in his chest, weeping uncontrollably. Slater squeezed me tighter while stroking my hair away from my face. "Oh, Sabela, I should never have left you alone. I'm so sorry."

I shook my head in protest. "No, Slater. This is not your fault. You can't be with me one hundred percent of the time. Davin would have found a way to get to me, one way or another. The guy is sick. I honestly think he snapped." I sniffed back my tears. "I don't know what would have happened if you hadn't barged in. I couldn't fight him." My tears became heavier as I relived what had just happened. "He was choking me with his arms."

Slater could see I was getting worked up again and consoled me with his soothing voice. "Shhh. It's over now. You're safe. He'll never hurt you again, I promise."

I raised my head and glanced over at Davin sprawled across the floor. "What do you think will happen to him?"

Slater reached into his pocket and pulled out his cell phone. "We'll let the cops decide that," he said as he dialed 9-1-1.

Still embraced by Slater's arms, I listened as he told the police what happened and gave them the address to where we were. In the back of my mind, a question kept haunting me.

Was this really over?

CHAPTER 25

SLATER

$\mathcal{M}$y biggest fears happened that morning. Everything I had been protecting Sabela from came true. When I entered that room, I became afraid of my own anger. I had no self-control and knew I would do anything to protect her, even if it meant killing the guy. I've never found myself in such a situation before. Sure, I've had fistfights with guys, but it was normally when I was drunk or just had a stupid disagreement with a friend or something. We made up soon after, and laughed and joked about the whole thing.

But this guy had tormented us, stalked us, and fucked with our lives, and as I was hitting him with all my strength, I was wishing he was dead. My anger scared me. If I hadn't knocked him out, I may have continued to hit him until I had killed him. There was no way Sabela could have stopped me. I would have been dragged off to jail in handcuffs, awaiting trial for murder or manslaughter. I couldn't even begin to think what that would have done to Sabela.

After calling the cops and explaining the whole thing to them, I called Drew and gave him the rundown on what happened, while keeping one eye on Davin, making sure he didn't begin to stir. After apologizing profusely and feeling somewhat responsible for hiring the guy, Drew said he'd be right over to give the cops his side of the story.

Sabela hadn't moved from the corner. Still haunted by the ordeal, she sat curled up with her knees under her chin, holding her legs tight and weeping, her head buried in her chest. It broke my heart to see her that way. Once off the phone, I sat down beside her and wrapped her in my arms as I tried to soothe her. Welcoming my embrace, she let her tears fall, drenching my shirt as she hid her face in my chest. I held her tight as she trembled, never wanting to let her go. I buried my face in her hair as the sounds of her sobbing tore at my heart.

In a way, I felt like I had failed her. I was supposed to be the one to protect her and prevent this from happening. I had done everything I possibly could to make sure Davin couldn't get to her, and yet he still had, and it was because I had left her alone.

Sabela and I had become too comfortable and let our guard down. Me more than her. I should have paid more attention to her fears of him showing up instead of trying to brush them off with accusations of her overreacting. As I held Sabela, lost in my own thoughts, I found myself drowning in guilt, wondering if Sabela would ever forgive me.

We waited in silence for help to arrive, stunned by what had just happened. No words were needed. I knew Sabela was safe now, and she knew it too. Our bodies were numb, and being in the comfort of each other's arms was what felt good right now.

Drew was the first one to arrive. I could tell he had raced over on foot. He almost fell through the open door, panting and wheezing to catch his breath. "You guys okay?" he managed to say before walking over to Davin and taking a good look at him.

I broke free from Sabela's hold, who struggled to let me go. I gave her a tight squeeze before rising to my feet. "I'll be right back."

My body ached as I stood. I held my stomach that what still

experiencing some pain. I wondered if I had some bruised ribs. I walked toward Drew, who was standing in the middle of the room, peering down at Davin.

"Yeah we're fine. Just banged up a little bit." I looked over at Sabela, who was now sitting up, her back against the wall. Thankfully, her tears had subsided. "Sabela is shook up, but I'll take care of her."

Drew continued to stare at Davin. "So, this is the asshole, eh?"

I nodded. "Yep."

Drew shook his head in disgust. "He was quite the smooth talker when I hired him yesterday. Said he'd been painting for years and he came across like he knew his stuff. I was short-handed, so I hired the guy." Drew swiped a hand down his face in disbelief. "Man, I never knew I was so bad at reading people.' He turned to me with wide eyes, his look apologetic. "I'm really sorry this happened. I had no idea this was your ex, Sabela," he said, glancing in her direction.

I gave him a friendly pat on the arm, "It's okay, man. You don't need to apologize. How were you to know?"

I didn't know Sabela was listening until I heard her speak in a broken voice. "Drew, it's not your fault. I'm just glad it's over." She began to sob again. "I'm so sorry this happened at work. He came in here with a mask on. I had no idea it was him. Only his eyes were showing."

I raced over to her before she became frantic again, and knelt beside her. "Shhh, it's okay. I told you, None, of this was your fault," I said, kissing her brow and holding her hands.

Trying to gain some composure, she shook her head and wiped away her new tears. "I know. I just can't believe what happened and what Davin did. I thought I knew him."

I remained next to her for a few minutes while Drew kept an eye on Davin. He had been out for a while, and I was expecting him to wake up any minute.

A few minutes later, two officers in uniform entered the room, both with their hands cradled over their weapons that hung from their hips. Relieved by their presence, I stood to greet them and extended my hand. "Officers, I can't tell you how happy I am to see you."

The heavier set officer shook my hand. "So, do you want to tell me what happened here?" he asked as they both walked over to Davin.

I pointed to the creep laying on the floor. "This man attacked my girlfriend. His name is Davin Haskell. He's been stalking her for weeks and—"

"Okay," the second officer cut me off. "Let's get this guy out of here first. Then we'll take down all your stories."

Drew stepped aside as he watched the officers begin to revive Davin to a conscious state by patting his cheeks.

Fearing how he would react once awake, Sabela instantly rose to her feet and

backed herself against the wall. I immediately sensed her nervousness and called out to the officers, as politely as I could, "Would you mind if she left the room until he is removed? She's been through enough already, and I don't want any more words exchanged between the two of them."

Not taking his eyes off Davin, one of the officers nodded. "Sure, that's fine. But we'll need to talk to her after we have this guy in custody, so don't have her go too far."

I turned to Drew. "Can you take her to the master bedroom for a few minutes? I'll come get you when he's gone." I then looked at Sabela. "You'll be fine with Drew," I told her while escorting her across the room into his arms.

I stood aside silently as I watched Davin begin to stir and moan. One of the cops had his handcuffs ready to snap onto his wrist, while the other continued to call his name. "Davin. Can you hear me? I need you to stand up. This is Officer Corral. Come on, Davin. Let's get you on your feet."

The heaviest and strongest of the officers stood behind Davin and pulled him to his feet by his armpits, into a standing position. "Come on. Up we go."

Davin shook his head in confusion. Dry blood caked his face and lip and he struggled to look over his shoulder at the officer. "What the fuck!" he yelled.

With a quick flip of his wrist, the officer immediately snapped the cuffs on Davin and quickly patted him down before leading him out of the room. "Come on, fella. You're coming with me."

Davin tried to resist the force the officer was using on him but there was no competition—the officer was almost twice his size and maneuvered him out of the room with ease, but not before Davin glared at me. "I'm going to get you, asshole. This isn't over."

I laughed at his stupidity. "Thanks for letting the cops know that, Davin."

The other cop butted in, "Okay, that's enough. Officer Beal will be getting his side of the story in the patrol car." He waited until the room was empty and then turned to me. "So, why don't you tell me what happened, and then I'll talk to your girlfriend and the other guy."

"That would be Drew. He's my boss. He hired the guy."

For the next twenty minutes, I told the cop everything I knew about Davin. I explained that he was Sabela's ex-boyfriend. How he had her thrown in jail, the harassing texts, and what happened today. Afterwards, he called in Sabela and Drew. I held Sabela in my arms as she told the cop everything. When she went into details of what had happened before I entered the room, she became emotional. It tore me up listening to her. Again, feelings of guilt swept through me for not being there.

When it was Drew's turn, he mentioned how I had asked him to hire Sabela and the reasons why. He went on to explain what a smooth talker Davin was and how he had tricked him into hiring him.

After we were finished, the cop said they had a good case against Davin and he

would be booked for attempted rape and other numerous charges. As I held Sabela, I felt her body relax in my arms. The words from the officer had finally brought some closure to the nightmare she had been enduring. She knew Davin could no longer hurt her and, to my surprise, when the officer turned to her and asked if she'd be willing to testify, she held her head high and simply said, "Absolutely."

I had never been more proud of her than at that very moment.

Before leaving, the cop shook our hands and told us he'd be in touch. Sabela was the first to thank him. I could see the relief shining in her eyes as she approached the officer and grasped his hand, shaking it profusely. All the fears she had been carrying for so many months were finally being washed away. I was finally seeing a genuine smile and it brought me so much comfort. I knew from that moment on, Sabela and I could finally get on with our lives.

Drew remained in the room after the officer had left. A look of disbelief blanketed his face as he spoke to us, "Again, I'm so sorry this happened to you, Sabela. I feel somewhat responsible for hiring the guy. I'm sorry I had no idea."

Sabela, refused to accept his apology and shook her head in protest. "No, Drew. Please don't. Like you said, you had no idea. The only person to blame is goddamn Davin."

Drew nodded. "You're right." He paused for a moment. "Listen. Why don't you guys take the rest of the day off. You've both been through a lot. Go home and get some rest. This can wait till tomorrow."

His suggestion brought a smile to our faces. "Thanks, Drew, I appreciate it." I took Sabela's hand. "Are you okay with that?" I asked.

"Yes, thank you, Drew. I want nothing more than to go home and take a shower."

Drew and I snuck a quick glance at each other. We both understood her desperate need to wash her body and simply nodded before gathering up my tools and calling it a day.

CHAPTER 26

SABELA

*W*hen Officer Corral asked me if I wanted to testify in court, there was no doubt in my mind when I told him yes. Davin could no longer hurt me and I'd be damned if I'd allow him to hurt some other woman because I was too scared to stand up to his bullying. If they called on me to testify against him, I'd go to court with my head held high and look directly at Davin as I described to the courts what he did to me. He would know I wasn't there for my own gratification, but for all the other women that may have been a victim of his.

As I rode home with Slater, my head in his lap and his fingers gently stroking my arm, I felt different. The fog had been lifted and the future was looking somewhat brighter. There was no longer a cloud of fear hanging over me. The realization the nightmare I had been living had finally come to an end drained my mind of all the terrifying thoughts I had suppressed and kept from Slater. I had this gut feeling Davin would come back to California and try to harm me in some way, and I was right. I couldn't blame Slater for thinking I was overreacting, but I'd always listened to my gut and it always proved me right.

As I lay in silence, numb from what had just taken place, images of Davin pressed against my body and choking me with his arm kept flashing in my head. I wondered what would have happened if Slater hadn't barged into the room. How far would Davin have gone? I was on the brink of passing out when he began to molest me. I shuddered at the thought, and my body jerked as I tried to wash the images away.

Concerned by my sudden movement, Slater stroked my hair away from my face and looked down. "Hey, are you okay?"

I rubbed his thigh through his jeans. "Yeah, I'm okay. I'm just thankful you came in the room when you did. God knows what would have happened if you didn't." I looked up toward his beautiful face. "Thank you."

"You don't have to thank me, silly. I'm just glad you're okay. I was ready to kill the guy."

"I know. I saw the fury in your eyes. And to be honest, I wouldn't care if you did."

Slater let out a little chuckle and squeezed my shoulder. I felt safe once more. I couldn't wait to get home and take a shower. The only thing left to do was wash my body of Davin's wretched scent, which I could still smell lingering over my entire body and, at times, made me gag.

Twenty minutes later, we pulled in to our parking space and in a mad dash, I grabbed my purse and hurried to the duplex without waiting for Slater. Once inside, I threw my purse on the couch, kicked off my tennis shoes, and began undressing before I had reached the bathroom. Leaving a trail of jeans, my top, and underwear behind me, I raced to the shower. I pulled open the door and turned the water on as hot as my skin could tolerate. I wanted to steam clean my entire body, scrub it clean of any remnants of Davin that may be lingering.

Once under the spray of steaming water, I became still, allowing the water to wash away the ghosts of Davin. I stared down at the drain and watched the water spin in circles, disap-

pearing and taking all the filth of Davin with it. I closed my eyes
and held my face up under the shower head. It almost felt like my
mind was being cleansed too. Tears began to mist my eyes. I let
them form and trickle down my cheeks. Before I knew it, I was
sobbing hard while wrapping my arms around myself. I reached
for the soap and lathered every inch of my body, making sure no
scent of Davin was left behind. Using both hands, I scrubbed my
skin with force, rubbing deep into my pores until they no longer
itched with the filth I was feeling.

I don't know how long I was in there, but I know it was for
quite a while. I had used half a bar of soap and had no more tears
left to cry. I was thankful Slater had not come in. I knew he sensed
I needed to be alone. He understood me well. When I was ready to
be touched by another man, he would know. But not now.

After I rinsed my body, I remained under the water for a few
more minutes. I had to make sure I was squeaky clean, and stood
in the pool of sudsy water with my eyes closed, trying desperately
to block the images of Davin that kept haunting my mind. I knew
it was going to take some time for the horrific memories to fade,
but I had Slater to help me replace them. The thought comforted
me and brought a smile to my face.

Satisfied I was clean, I turned off the water and instantly
became chilled. Clenching my hands in front of my chest to block
the cold air, I quickly stepped out of the shower, dried off with a
towel, and wrapped myself in my bathrobe, snuggling my face into
the thick fuzzy fleece collar. I glanced at myself in the mirror. My
eyes were red and swollen from my tears, my skin was pale, and
my hair was a tangled mess, but I was too tired to brush it. Fatigue
was overpowering my body. I didn't know how much longer I
could stand on my legs that felt weak and were beginning to
tremble.

I still had the need to be alone and chose not to go out to the
living room. Instead, I headed for the bedroom and sought the
comfort of the bed. Still wrapped in my bathrobe, I crawled under

the covers and pulled the quilt up high under my chin. The warmth soothed me as I felt myself slowly drifting off to sleep.

~

"No!" I didn't know how long I had been sleeping, but I woke in a panicked state, my body soaked with sweat. I bolted up out of a deep sleep to find Slater sitting next to me, holding on to my hand.

"Shhh, it's okay. It's just a nightmare," I heard him say.

Seeing Slater next to me snapped me back to reality. I was home in my bed, safe. It was just a dream. Davin was not here. I clung to Slater, my head limp in his lap. "Oh God, Slater, I'm so happy to see you. I dreamt Davin was here. I couldn't stop him. He was about to—" I stopped myself. "God, it was horrible."

While I was sleeping, I had obviously been crying. My pillow was wet and my face was drenched. I curled my body tight, close to Slater. His strong arms cradled me as I let the horrors of the nightmare subside.

"It's okay. Nothing is going to happen to you now. You've just had a bad dream."

His words comforted me. He was right, Davin could no longer hurt me. I had the protection of the law, and Slater and I would do everything in my power to make sure he was locked up behind bars for a long time.

Slater and I made love that night. It was magical and beautiful. We both had a burning desire to become one and pledge our deepest love for each other. He treated me like fine china. His touch was gentle, his kisses delicate and soft. He moved slow, caressing me with tender featherlike strokes until I gave myself completely to him. I melted beneath him like hot wax until our bodies became one.

I knew at the precise moment when he entered me, I was where I was meant to be. There was no other man for me and I knew there was no other woman for him. He laid on top me, our bodies tangled, his thrusts gentle. Neither one of us was in a hurry to climax. In silence, we talked only with our eyes, gazing and mesmerized by each other as we felt the comfort of our naked bodies embracing as one. With baited breath, we kissed passionately, exploring each other's mouths and lips with our tongues. When we came, it was together as we held each other close, burying our heads in each other's chest as we moaned with pleasure. Our bodies peaked to a climatic state before we slowly collapsed into each other's arms.

I realized then, I had my life back and I was going to be okay. Sweating and out of breath, with Slater slumped on top of me, his head laying on my chest, I no longer feared Davin. He would soon be a distant memory that could no longer hurt me. As I lay there rendering the thought, gushes of heat swept through me, giving me a warm cozy feeling. I smiled to myself and wrapped my arms around Slater, squeezing him tight. I looked down at his beautiful ruffled hair, the scent captured in my nose, and I buried my face in his hair. "I love you, Slater."

"God, I love you too, Sabela," he replied with his eyes still closed.

CHAPTER 27

SABELA

Over the next few weeks, life slowly began to return to normal. The weekend after the incident with Davin, Slater and I drove out to my mother's house for another visit. But this time, with Davin locked up in jail, I decided to come clean and tell her everything. At first, she was offended I hadn't told her sooner but once I had expressed my fears, she understood and her concerns were replaced with anger toward Davin. She praised me when I told her I would testify and said I got my strength from my father. With tears in her eyes, she told me I was doing the right thing and that Dad would be watching over me.

There was another reason for our visit. Both Slater and I had an urgency to move. The duplex was, and always would be, the place I had shared with Davin. It no longer felt like home to me and never did for Slater. It was a place filled with memories I soon would like to forget. Living there was keeping us in the past and we both desperately wanted to move forward and build a future together.

Since I'd met Slater, we'd been living from paycheck to paycheck, barely making the rent. How were we suppose to come up with the cash to get a new place? We couldn't even save any money. That's when I had the idea of moving in with my mom. At first, Slater didn't like the idea. I think his pride got in the way. A man is supposed to take care of his woman, he explained, and he was also afraid what my mom would think of him. He didn't want to lose the high respect she currently had for him. After I reassured Slater my mother adored him and she'd probably love our company after losing Dad, he soon warmed up to the idea, but not without insisting we pay our way. I agreed, knowing it would be far cheaper than living at the duplex, and we could finally begin saving some money toward a place of our own with no history. The only setback would be our commute to work—instead of being twenty minutes, it would now be at least hour, but that was far better than remaining at the duplex.

When I approached my mom about our idea, she couldn't say yes fast enough. It was the first time I had seen her genuinely happy since Dad died and it brought tears to my eyes as she jumped out of her chair and danced circles around the room. She raised her arms with joy, with all kinds of enthusiastic plans to fix up the spare room. Both Slater and I laughed as we watched her and celebrated with a homemade lasagna dinner cooked by Mom and me before heading home to begin packing.

I knew I didn't want most of the furniture because I had bought it with Davin, and decided I would donate it to the Salvation Army, leaving us to only pack our clothes and personal items. That would only take a few days.

To get my deposit back, which would be the roots for our savings, I'd have to give the landlord thirty days' notice, which wasn't an issue. Not wanting to be at the duplex any longer than necessary, we planned on moving in with my mother the following weekend. We figured we wouldn't tell the landlord, and the apartment would just remain empty until the end of the month.

When we returned home, anxious to begin packing, Officer Corral called me with some surprising developments in the case against Davin. Apparently, two other women from the University in Texas had come forward, accusing him of rape, and were willing to testify. I was stunned and wondered if there were any victims here in California and if there were, did Davin commit the crime when he was with me? The thought that there was a possibility horrified me. I knew now, without a doubt, the State had a strong case and Davin would be going away for some time, with the help of myself and the other two women. A date for the trial had not been set yet, but feeling triumphant, I told Officer Corral I was ready and would do whatever it took to make sure he couldn't hurt anyone else. Officer Corral admired my courage and told me the department would be behind me one hundred percent and would be in touch soon.

The next day, I had a long conversation over the phone with the prosecuting attorney who I was thankful was a woman. As uncomfortable as this already was, the thought of being questioned by a man about the sordid details would make it much worse. She told me, with all the evidence they had against Davin, it was pretty much an open-and-shut case, and it should be a quick trial. She also talked to Slater and asked if he would be willing to testify if needed. Even though it wasn't needed to persuade him to say yes, she mentioned to him Drew would be testifying too.

It didn't take us long to pack. We were finished in two days. They only thing left to do was wait for the Salvation Army to come pick up the furniture. They were scheduled to be here in an hour, around four. We had left work earlier so we could be here on time, and while we waited, we loaded up the truck with all the items we were taking to my mom's. I knew it wouldn't be a problem telling Mom we would be moving in before the weekend. She was as excited as we were, if not more.

When we were finally on our way, I left Slater to lock up the duplex. I had no goodbyes, no cherished memories of the place. I was done and didn't even look back as Slater locked the door. As we walked away, it felt like a fresh of breath air had swept over me.

I took Slater's hands, gave him a warm smile, and skipped to the truck, excited about beginning a new life with him.

The only part of my past life that had any attachments was the upcoming trial. But I was prepared. I wanted to testify and stop Davin, and I knew I was going to be okay.

CHAPTER 28

*M*oving into Sabela's mother's house wasn't as bad as I had anticipated. Charlotte welcomed me like I was her own son. In no time at all, we were living like one big, happy family. I tried to help around the house as much as I could during the evenings after work. There were many repairs needed since Sabela's father passed away, and Sabela and I even pulled out the old carpet from the spare bedroom and laid down a new hardwood floor. Her mother was quite impressed with her daughter's newfound skills in construction, and even mentioned to Sabela she should forget about dentistry because Sabela and I made a great team.

I must admit, for a few days, it felt odd not having Sabela at my side twenty-four seven. For so long, I had feared a surprise visit from Davin—which, ironically did happen—I was afraid to let her out of my sight. Now, we were living like a normal couple, both free to come and go as we pleased. It took some getting used to and if she left the house, I'd find myself sweating with worry until she returned safely. But the anxieties were beginning to fade and

we were slowly settling into our new life together. It's friggin'
awesome.

~

I t took eight months for the trial to begin and it was a somber
evening on the eve of the first day. We were still living with her
mother, which was what Sabela wanted. She needed the comforts
of the home where she grew up, and that of her mother. Both
Charlotte and I were worried about Sabela, who wasn't saying
much. She just seemed so calm and reserved, keeping to herself
most of the night by taking a long bath and turning in early to read
a book.

When asked first by me and then her mother, an hour later, if
she was okay, she replied with a soft smile and confirmed she was,
that she was just gathering her thoughts together in preparation
for tomorrow. Not wanting to pursue the matter or upset her,
Charlotte and I understood how hard this must be for her and
gave her the space she needed.

Neither Sabela nor I could sleep well that night, it came in
spurts. At 3:00 a.m., I woke to find the bed empty. In a panicked
state, I jumped out of the bed in search for her. A few minutes
later, I found her sitting outside on the patio in her black silk pajamas, looking up at the dark skies. Not wanting to startle her, I slid
the glass door open slowly and joined her. "Hey, are you okay?" I
whispered.

She gave me a sleepy smile, which told me I wasn't intruding.
"Yeah, I'm fine. I just couldn't sleep."

I sat beside her in the empty chair and took her hand. "I know,
me too." For the next

few minutes, an awkward silence fell between us as we both sat
gazing at the moon high up in the sky. Can I get you anything?"

"No, I'm good. I just needed some fresh air. I woke up
sweating."

I coughed before I spoke. "Are you sure you're going to be okay tomorrow? I know I've asked you so many times, but I'm worried about you. It's not going to be easy to get up on the stand and talk about what happened." I paused. "You've not really talked about it much. You've be keeping to yourself a lot lately."

She stopped looking at the moon and instead focused on our hands resting on the
arm of her chair, tangled together. She stroked her thumb back and forth across my hand. "I'm sorry. I didn't mean to avoid you or Mom. I have so much crap buzzing around in my head right now, and I'm just trying to deal with it the best way I can. I'm not sure what to expect tomorrow, but I do know this." She turned to me, her eyes wide. "I will walk into that courtroom like my life depended on it. I will use every bit of inner strength that I can muster up, and I will tell the courts everything Davin did to me, and in detail, if I must."

Sabela moved her face closer to mine. "I will look him in the eyes when I do. It will be a stare that will pierce him and haunt him for the rest of his life. He will feel his skin crawl and the hairs on the back of his neck will stand straight up. I want to see him squirm in his seat. I want to see him look away, because I will not. As long as I'm testifying on that stand, I will be looking at that snake of a person. And when I watch him being carted off to jail, for what I hope will be many years, my smile will finally become a joyous one, which will radiate throughout the entire courtroom."

Listening to her talk with such determination and courage gave me goose bumps. I knew then she was going to be okay. Me, on the other hand, I wasn't so sure. How was I going to handle watching Sabela testify? I felt so helpless. In a way, I was hoping they would call me to the stand. At least if they did, I would feel like I was contributing. Right now, the only thing I could do was give her moral support, but it seemed so inadequate for what was expected of her by the courts.

The next morning, I woke at six, alone in the bed, feeling tired from staying out on the deck with Sabela until the early hours. From the hallway, I heard the shower running. Images of her wet and naked body shadowed my mind as I rubbed my morning stiffy. I quickly scolded myself. "Come on, Slater. Stop fucking around. It's an important day."

With an urgency and wanting to have a sense of responsibility, I lifted my tired body from the bed and headed downstairs to make coffee for everyone.

Twenty minutes later, already dressed in a navy-blue skirt and matching jacket, with a white shirt, Charlotte appeared first and made a beeline for the coffee. Initially, Sabela had not wanted her mother to go to the trial and be exposed to any of the sordid details that may come out. But her mother stood her ground and scolded Sabela for trying to stop her from supporting her daughter. Sabela knew she couldn't argue with that and reluctantly agreed.

A few minutes later, Sabela made her way down the stairs. She looked magnificent in her black pants suit and white shirt. Her hair was neatly tied back in a ponytail. She descended the stairs with a look of confidence and strength. She approached me and gave me a light kiss on the lips. "Why are you not dressed?" she asked.

I looked down at my bathrobe attire. "What's wrong with it. It's all the rage, I hear," I joked, trying to add humor to what was going to be an emotional day for all of us.

Sabela chuckled, appreciating the joke before slapping me on the backside. "Get upstairs and get dressed. We have to leave in half an hour."

I threw her a wink followed by a salute. "Yes, ma'am," and I quickly scurried up the stairs to shower and change.

Because Charlotte's car had more room than my truck, we opted to take her car. We arrived with plenty of time to spare, and to talk to the prosecuting attorney and the officers, where I found out I would be called to testify. I was stunned at first, silenced by a lump in my throat, but this is what I had wanted—to be more than just another member of the audience. I vigorously shook the attorney's hand with gratitude.

"Sure. Sure. No problem. I won't let you down," I said, while my heart pounded in my chest with the accelerated nerves I was now feeling.

She also mentioned both the prosecutor and defendants were allowing all witnesses to be present in the courtroom for the entire trial, something that was not common but magically, our attorney made it happen. I released a huge sigh of relief, knowing I could be close by when Sabela gave her testimony. I knew she felt the same way by the way she squeezed my hand and gave me a loving smile.

When Davin was brought into the courtroom, handcuffed and dressed in an orange jumpsuit, escorted by two officers, it took all my strength and willpower not to release all the rage I was feeling just by the mere sight of him. Feeling Sabela's body shudder against me, I wrapped my arm tightly around her shoulders and pulled her in close, noticing the sudden chill that now clouded the air from his presence, except for his sister, Claire, and his parents, who released pathetic cries from the front. I shook my head in disgust.

After the prosecutor had presented their case, they called on the other two victims first, and then Sabela, to testify. It was heart-wrenching to listen to their stories and watch one of the women break down on the stand as she relived the horrible night Davin raped her and penetrated her by force. The realization Davin probably wouldn't have stopped attacking Sabela if I hadn't entered the room hit me hard. When I looked over at Davin as these women opened their wounds that were caused by him, I became even more revolted by his presence. He showed no signs of remorse and just sat there with a slimy smirk smeared across his face.

When Sabela's name was called, she sucked in a deep breath and turned to me with misty eyes. For a minute, I thought she was going to lose it, but she didn't. Instead, she squeezed my hand tight and whispered, "I'm fine."

For the next thirty minutes, I watched with the utmost pride as Sabela held it together and told the courts everything—from their previous relationship to their goodbyes at the airport, the harassing texts and his false car theft accusation that landed her in jail for three days, and then the horrifying attempted rape incident. She did exactly what she said she was going to do and stared at Davin the whole time. A few times, I saw him squirm in his seat and look away. God, what a satisfying feeling that was.

After her testimony was over, I could tell Sabela was struggling with her emotions by the way she stumbled off the stand, but I knew she refused to let Davin see her crumble before him. She managed to hold it together and not shed a tear while she walked back to her seat, where she snuggled into my side.

Drew and I were next on the stand. Drew talked about the time I had called him, asking him to hire Sabela and the reasons why. He then went on and told the courts about the day Davin came into his office, looking for work, and being short-staffed, he hired him on the spot. And how he immediately sought out Sabela and assaulted her.

After Drew, my name was called. I squeezed Sabela's hand before giving her a

quick kiss on the top of the head and walked toward the stand. During my testimony, I glanced a couple of times over at Davin, but he disgusted me too much and instead, found myself fixated on Sabela.

I told the courts about the texts, which were produced as evidence from the screenshots I had taken, and how she had called me when she was released from jail. When it came to describe the incident at work where I had to pull Davin off Sabela and defend not only her but also myself, I immediately felt my blood begin to boil and my face became flushed with anger. I didn't say his name,

I *spat* his name, as I pointed to him with my eyes narrowed and my lips curled in disgust. "That is the man that did this."

I was the last person to speak that day and the final witness for the prosecutors. We were thankful to hear Davin would not be taking the stand. Tomorrow, the defense attorney, who was a male, would present their case.

CHAPTER 29

SABELA

*W*hen my name was called to take the stand, I didn't just walk through the courtroom—I marched with the attitude and strength of an entire army, determined not to be taken down or intimated by my enemy. This was the only chance I was going to have to protect myself and other women from the monster who sat before me, and I was going to be damn sure everyone heard me. As far as I was concerned, there was just me, Davin, and the prosecutor in the room. I blocked out every other person and sound as I told my story.

With my inner strength guiding me, and feeling the presence of my dad looking down upon me, I focused the rage I was feeling deep inside my gut into the piercing stare I fixed on Davin throughout my entire time on the stand. I wasn't going to give him the satisfaction of seeing any tears shed or my body crumble before him. I remained poised and alert, not leaving out any details of the torment I had endured by him for the past few months. I knew my dad would have been proud of me.

I didn't cower beneath the questioning of the defense attorney, who tried his best to twist everything I had said and convince the courts it was my actions that had caused Davin to act the way he did.

"Isn't true to say that you were upset with Davin for leaving you and that you did steal his car and he had come back to California to retrieve it from impound?" The prosecutor said while peering at me over his glasses.

I snarled at him with gritted teeth as I spoke in my defense, wondering how a person can find gratification from defending a criminal. "No that is not true. I did not steal his car; he gave it to me." A horrifying thought suddenly popped into my head. *How many criminals are now free because of this man?*

"Then please explain why Davin still has the pink slip." The prosecutor said.

I was horrified that this man was treating me like I was the criminal here. His questions were just ludicrous. I clenched my fists around the wooden handles of my chair to help surpress the anger I was feeling. "He forgot to give it to me before he left for Texas. I was going to call him and ask him to mail it to me but then he started harassing me."

The prosecuting attorney released a sarcastic grin. "Is that so Miss Hutchinson?"

He continued to twist the story through his absurd questioning but each time I came back with a vengeance.

The trial lasted three days, after which it was in the hands of the jury, which consisted of eight women and four men. The prosecutor felt confident they would return quickly with a guilty verdict. She was right—they returned within less than an hour with what she had predicted, and found Davin guilty on two counts of aggravated rape and one count of sexual assault. He was also charged with making a false car theft claim. When the charges were read, an exuberant number of tears of joy were shed between my mom and me as Slater held us tight. We clung together as each charge was read, rejoicing at each verdict. My day in court had finally come.

Even though the sentencing trail would not be held for a few more weeks, the prosecutor assured us he was facing ten to twenty years in prison, which brought more tears. I knew now, I was finally safe.

It was only when the verdict was read that I allowed my tears to fall. Not wanting them to be mistaken for anything but tears of joy and triumphant, I added a cheer while directing my winning smile solely at Davin. Watching him quickly turn away with his head hung low was the most gratifying sight to witness.

During the entire trial, I hadn't spoken to the other victims, but our teary eyes met instantly from across the courtroom when the guilty verdicts were called. From our seats, we watched with an exuberant amount of joy as Davin was escorted out of the room in handcuffs. At that moment, I wanted to share the glorious triumph with the other women, and broke free from my mother and Slater's embrace.

"Will you excuse me for a minute?" I quietly said, looking over at one of the women who was also looking at me. When she noticed I was walking in her direction, she broke away from the embrace of an older male, who I assumed was her father, and walked toward me with tears streaming down her face.

As the distance between us shortened, anxious to celebrate together, our paces quickened until we were face to face in the aisle. Did she notice the uncanny resemblance between us? We both had long black hair and natural olive-toned skin. Our build was identical. I was then reminded of Davin's comment, before he assaulted me. When he attacked these women, he was thinking they were me, and took his rage out on them.

For a moment, we just stood and stared at each other, overwhelmed with emotions, our eyes flooded with endless tears. Neither one of us could speak but we didn't need to—the expressions painted on our faces said it all. At the same time, we opened our arms and welcomed each other, holding one another tight as the words, "Thank you!" were whispered.

A short time after, I felt a hand on my shoulder and the sound of tears. I raised my head and saw the other victim beside us with tears gushing down her face. She too had the same features as myself and the other woman. I lifted my arm and welcomed her into our circle, where we remained silent and only the sounds of our crying could be heard.

When we finally broke away, I held their hands tight before thanking them one more time and saying goodbye. There was no talk of keeping in touch. Deep down, I sensed we all knew if we did, it would only stir up memories of this horrific time in our lives and keep us living in the past. We all needed to move forward without looking back, and we all knew the true purpose of why we were brought together.

A few weeks later, Davin was sentenced to fifteen years in jail. I did not attend the sentencing hearing, nor did Slater or my mom. My job was done and I had seen what I had wanted, which was the back of Davin, handcuffed and exiting the courtroom on his way to jail. I had begun to pick up the pieces and heal from the wounds I had endured. Returning to the courts would only re-open some of those wounds and I refused to allow that to happen.

Life was finally returning to the way it was when I first met Slater almost a year ago. We were still living with my mom, in no rush to move while we had waited for the trial to begin. I had needed to be close to her and have her support. Luckily, the job with the condos had been extended, and Slater and I knew we had work for the next six months. We had managed to save enough money to get our own place, but we weren't ready to leave just yet.

I was feeling almost back to normal, with the wounds of the past now buried. But there was something I had discovered about myself when I first met Slater, and I needed to know if I could still enjoy it the way I did before everything happened. If I could, then I knew I had truly won and Davin could no longer haunt me. It was time to approach Slater with my crazy idea, while enjoying a glass of wine and the sunset from the back deck at my mom's house.

With a devious smile, I turned to him, sitting in the deck chair next to me. Before speaking, I took a sip of wine. "You know, we haven't been to the beach since before the trial."

"I know. With everything that has happened, I didn't think it was a good time to mention it. You've needed your space and a time to heal. It's been a busy and emotional time for the two of us."

I circled the rim of my glass. "Well, we're not busy now. In fact, tomorrow is Saturday. We have the whole day to do whatever we want." Still wearing my devious smile, I set down my glass, rose from my chair, and took a seat on Slater's lap. I wrapped my arms around his neck. "I think we need some alone time at the beach. Just you and me." I rolled my eyes in a mischievous manner. "And whoever else might show up."

A look of surprise covered Slater's face. "Wait! Are you suggesting what I think you are?"

I cocked my head back as I laughed. "I might be."

Slater was on to what I was getting at. "You want to do what we did at the beach when we first met, don't you?" he asked, with a stunned look on his face. "You want people to watch us. Am I right?"

"I think it will be fun." I giggled. "This may sound crazy, but I need to know if the ghosts of Davin have finally left me. I discovered the fun of being watched with you and got so turned on by the whole thing before Davin started messing with my life. I want to start enjoying it again. We had so much fun doing it. I want life to be the way it was when I first met you, and that is part of it." I nudged his arm. "Come on, Slater. Let's do it. It's about time we had some fun."

Slater shook his head in disbelief. "Are you sure you're ready? I'd love to. I love showing you off."

"Yes, I'm ready. I've been cooped up in this shell of fear for too long. It's time to break free and live my life again."

Slater hooked the back of my neck with his hand and pulled me in close before kissing me passionately on the lips. "Okay. Let's go to the beach tomorrow."

CHAPTER 30

SABELA

Sabela

*I*t was already beginning to feel like old times. After packing our bags and an ice chest—and even Slater's surfboard, which he hadn't used since Davin's arrest—we arrived at the beach early, around 9:00. It was a different beach, only twenty minutes from my mom's house, but I hoped we would eventually make it *our* beach.

The sun was already beginning to shine its powerful rays upon us, and I was soon sweating beneath my clothes. There weren't too many people on the sand at this hour, but I knew that would change as the day grew hotter. The ocean, however, was populated with an abundance of surfers, sitting on their boards, waiting for the next big wave. As we walked across the beach, Slater turned and looked in their direction. "Oh man, it's gonna feel good to surf again."

"You should go in after we've found our spot. I want to catch some rays anyways."

It warmed my heart to see the smile on Slater's face return. It had been so long since I had seen it. It was a genuine, real smile that wasn't forced, and I already knew this trip to the beach was a good idea.

After finding a secluded spot close to the rocks, away from where crowds might gather, we laid out our towels and I watched as Slater anxiously stripped down and slid into his wetsuit. As he stood there before me, carrying his surfboard, his wetsuit hugging every lean muscle on his body, it reminded me of the first time I met him. He was just as sexy now as he was back then. I watched with admiration as he scurried across the sand toward the ocean for a long overdue surfing session.

Once Slater became a blurb amongst the other surfers in the water, I began to undress. I peeled my jeans off my body, leaving only my white bikini bottoms. Periodically, I caught myself scanning the beach for any eyes that may be looking my way as I undressed and a flutter of disappointment reached inside of me when I did not. *It's still early,* I told myself. I reached up high to the sky and pulled my pink t-shirt over my head, tossing it by my feet. I stood there for a while, soaking up the rays and enjoying the warmth coating my skin. It had been a while since it had been exposed to the sun and it was obvious. Even though I was naturally dark-skinned, it didn't have the deep brown tone I liked.

Before lying down, I glanced out toward the ocean to see if I could see Slater but the surfers all looked alike in their black wetsuits, sitting on their boards, and I gave up. After smoothing out my towel with my feet, I took my spot, put on my favorite oversized sunglasses, and stretched out on my back with my legs slightly apart. Instantly, the heat generated from the sun soothed me and I released a loud sigh of comfort as I closed my eyes and allowed my body to bake.

I'm not sure how long I had been laying there, but I must have dozed off because I was awoken by cold droplets of water hitting my stomach. I opened my eyes and looked up. Standing over me was Slater, smiling. His hair was a matted mess and continued to drip onto my skin.

"Man. You look fine lying there," he said as he shook his head vigorously above me, causing a shower of drops to hit my stomach.

I winched and laughed. "Oooh, that's cold."

Slater laughed at my reaction as he began to remove his wetsuit and lay it out flat on a towel to dry. "Mind if I join you?"

I patted the towel and scooched over to make room for him. "Come on," I said, while being reminded of our first encounter.

Slater scanned the beach. "Looks like a few more people have showed up. I wonder how many have been admiring your perfect body?" He reached over my shoulder and grabbed the bottle of coconut oil. I breathed in his delicious scent as his arm passed over me. "Only one way to find out. I bet a few of the single guys out there would love to watch me smear this oil all over your gorgeous skin."

I giggled as a twinge of excitement stirred deep inside of me at the thought. I closed my eyes in anticipation and took in a sharp deep breath as I felt the warmth of the oil trickle over my belly. I moaned with pleasure when I felt Slater's masculine hands glide over my heated skin with deep, massaging strokes.

"God, you're beautiful," he whispered as he poured more oil between the V of my breasts. I gasped as the oil trickled beneath my top and Slater followed the oil with his hands, smearing it across the top of the mounds of my chest and sliding them deep inside my bikini top. I arched my back as he cupped my breasts in his hands and teased my nipples that were now beginning to get hard from his touch.

"Don't look up, but we have an onlooker at three o'clock. He just scooched his towel closer and is within twenty feet of us," Slater murmured close to my ear.

"Really?" I whispered as I arched my back even more.

"I just gave him a friendly grin. He knows we're cool."

Slater continued to massage my breasts and with every stroke, he slowly revealed another inch of my skin until they were barely covered by the material of my bikini top. I tossed my head back and forth from the sensations rushing through my body, both from his touch and thinking of our new friend watching our every move. I was on fire and didn't want him to stop. I was panting, my chest heaving, and Slater had to silence me with his lips. Pressing hard, filled with passion, he smothered my mouth with his, circling his tongue with mine. His breath was refreshing, coated with the scent of the ocean.

While still locked in a kiss, Slater traced the curves of my body down to my thighs and gently pulled my legs apart. I gasped between breaths of his kiss as I felt his fingertips curl around the edges of my bikini bottom and into my now drenched core. I spread my legs a little wider. I wanted our audience to see the joy I was experiencing. That's what turned me on so much. Not only Slater's touch but the other eyes upon us, wishing they were Slater and doing what he was doing to me.

Using the utmost discretion—after all, we were on a public beach—Slater slid his finger deep inside of me. I moaned with pleasure while digging my nails into his back to soften my voice from the electrifying sensations I was experiencing.

"Feels good. Doesn't it?" Slater whispered before tracing the curves of my breast with his tongue.

"Yes." I moaned.

Slater inched his finger deeper inside my core. I spread my legs a little further to welcome him and moved my hips in a gentle circular motion, grinding on his hand.

He kissed my neck—his breath was warm—and he worked his way back up to my lips with soft, sensual kisses. Breathing heavily, he looked into my eyes and whispered, "Do you want me to make you come? I bet our new friend would love to watch you squeal with ecstasy. He's moved a little closer. Let's give him a show."

I was now panting uncontrollably. Taking in quick short breaths and grinding my body against his, I begged, "Yes. Make me come."

No sooner had I given Slater the okay, he began pumping me with his finger using a fast, rhythmic motion, while kissing me deeply to soften my louder moans. Every nerve ending in my body was on fire, charged by the electrifying rush shooting through my bloodstream. This is what I had wanted and I was ecstatic Davin hadn't stripped me of this pleasure I had discovered with Slater. The animal was still inside of me and I could release it whenever I choose.

I could feel the rush of an orgasm approaching. My head was beginning to spin and my body was becoming tense with anticipation of letting the orgasm take over from deep inside my body. I braced for impact, held my breath, and felt it ignite between my legs. I gasped as it flowed and before I could scream at the top of my lungs, Slater covered my mouth entirely, pushing my head hard into the sand to smother the deafening sounds that were about to echo from my mouth.

Amid the overpowering orgasm, I dug my nails deep into his back, pulling him on top of me, and thrust my hips up to his hand that was buried between my legs. My body jolted in sharp jerks as the power of the climax began to subside, leaving me numb and my body tingling from head to toe. With my moans now less frequent and softer, Slater relaxed his kiss and removed his hand. "Wow!"

I raised my hand to cover my mouth and giggled like a little girl. "God, I feel fantastic."

Slater raised his head and turned to the stranger, giving him a simple smile. The man understood, rose to his feet and picked up his towel, and walked away without turning back.

"That must be a universal language between guys during these situations. Because he understood it was time to leave when you threw him a grin," I said with a laugh.

"Yep. It seems to work." Slater snickered.

Feeling completely relaxed and breathless, we remained in each other's arms for some time, allowing the heat from the sun to soothe us. In the distance, we could hear the rumble of the waves crashing against the shore, but other than that, it felt like it was just me and Slater.

"I love you, Sabela," Slater softly said, his head on my chest as he looked up to the sky.

"I love you too, Slater."

He turned to face me. His hair glistened in the sun. He was the most beautiful man I had ever known. He gave me a loving smile and kissed me tenderly on my lips before he spoke.

"I love you more than anything on this earth. I want to spend the rest of my life with you and take care of you." He paused and I gasped, anticipating his next words. He took my hand and smiled again. "Sabela, will you marry me?"

I squealed, "Yes!" before the happy tears began flowing uncontrollably down my face. I kept saying it while trying to brush away the tears of joy. "Yes! Yes!" In a rush of excitement, I rose to my knees to meet Slater, who was now on his. We faced each other, our noses touching, our palms entwined. "Yes, I'll marry you."

Slater pulled me in close before hugging me tight. "I can't wait to begin my life with you."

I rested my head on his chest. "I'm ready to find a home with you and plan our wedding with you and Mom." Thoughts of telling my mom the news excited me and I looked up at Slater, my eyes almost popping out of my head. "Wait till Mom hears we're getting married. Oh, I can't wait to see the look on her face."

Slater laughed. "The only thing that concerns me is our jobs. What are we going to do once the condos are built? We'll be out of work."

I rubbed his arms firmly, not wanting him to worry. "Slater, we'll figure something out. Don't fret over it now. I know, whatever we decide, it will be fantastic and we'll be good at it, and it will be something to look forward to." I gave him another reassuring smile. "In the meantime, let's go home and tell my mom we have a wedding to plan!"

The End of Book One

ABOUT THE AUTHOR

ABOUT THE AUTHOR

Tina Hogan Grant loves to write stories with strong female characters that know what they want and aren't afraid to chase their dreams. She loves to write sexy and sometimes steamy romances with happy ever after endings.

She is living life to the fullest in a small mountain community in Southern California with her husband and two dogs. When she is not writing she is probably riding her ATV, kayaking or hiking with her best friend – her husband of twenty-five years.

www.tinahogangrant.com

WHERE CAN YOU FIND TINA?

Join her Facebook Reading Group where she does live chats, cover reveals, reads excerpts and does plenty of giveaways including signed ACR books.

FOLLOW HER ON THESE SOCIAL MEDIA ACCOUNTS

CPSIA information can be obtained
at www.ICGtesting.com
Printed in the USA
FSHW010951050919
61609FS